The Nightmare on Trap Street

The Nightmare on Trap Street

C. N. Phillips

www.urbanbooks.net

Urban Books, LLC
300 Farmingdale Road, NY-Route 109
Farmingdale, NY 11735

The Nightmare on Trap Street

ISBN 13: 978-1-64556-363-1
ISBN 10: 1-64556-363-4

First Mass Market Printing August 2022
First Trade Paperback Printing September 2020
Printed in the United States of America

10 9 8 7 6 5 4 3 2 1

Distributed by Kensington Publishing Corp.
Submit Orders to:
Customer Service
400 Hahn Road
Westminster, MD 21157-4627
Phone: 1-800-733-3000
Fax: 1-800-659-2436

Chapter 1

"Pull over there, by that tunnel, and let me out."

The deep and demanding voice belonged to Cam Lewis, one of Detroit's big-time hustlers. He sat in the back seat of his Maybach and took notice of a black Mercedes already parked. He wasn't surprised, being as he was there to meet someone. However, that didn't mean he was happy to see the vehicle. Cam grabbed a duffle bag that was on the seat next to him and placed it on his lap. He unzipped it, and his eyes were instantly met with the green contents inside—$250,000, a payment that he owed and wasn't happy to be parting with. The vein protruding from his right temple showed that. Before blessing the ground with the Ferragamo loafers on his feet, he pulled a flip phone from his pocket and dialed a number.

"Hello?" Cam's young soldier Dwayne answered with a gruff voice.

"I'm here," Cam said.

"We see you."

"Everybody in position?"

"Yup. Whoever is in that tunnel won't be making it out of here alive, boss."

"Be sure of it," Cam instructed icily. "If everything goes as planned, you won't just be leaving here with some extra money in your pocket, but you'll have a new Mercedes, too."

He flipped the phone closed and cleared his throat. He looked up at Felix, his driver for the past five years, and nodded before putting the duffle bag strap on his shoulder. Felix got out and went around to open Cam's door. He stepped out and smoothed the jacket of his gray suit.

"I'll wait here," the older man said and tipped his hat.

"I shouldn't be long," Cam told him and started walking toward the tunnel's entrance.

They were in a construction zone. However, it had rained that summer day, and all of the workers had gone home, leaving behind all of the machinery and half-dug holes. Although it was midday, the sun was battling against the clouds to peek through.

The meeting for payment had been in motion for a few days, but the location was switched last minute. However, that didn't put an end to Cam's plan to not have to pay a dime. See, not only was he tired of having to go through a middleman to get his product, but he was tired of having his title on the streets capped at "lieutenant." He wasn't anyone's lieutenant. He was the boss, and it was time that Detroit knew that. Everyone knew that The Last Kings ruled over Detroit, but every reign came to an end sometime.

Some years back—when Khiron, a cat from Atlanta, had overthrown The Last Kings and taken over business in Detroit—Cam was much happier. He was given control over three territories and was eating good. However, when Khiron was killed and The Last Kings regained power over the streets, business went back to how it was before Khiron took over. Cam went back to his one territory. And that meant less money. The goal was for everybody to have a way to eat, but Cam couldn't be worried about the next mouth when his plate wasn't filled up. Growing up as the block's "brown-skinned pretty boy," Cam had grown accustomed to getting what he wanted. All he had to do was flash his perfectly straight teeth and follow that with some smooth talking. Now things were different. He had to take what he wanted.

Cam cleared his throat when he stepped into the shadows inside the tunnel. It was dim, but he could still clearly make out everything around him, like the woman in a form-fitting pantsuit and Christian Louboutin heels leaning against the cement wall, filing her nails.

"You're late," she said without looking up from what she was doing.

"My apologies, Sadie," Cam said, addressing the head of The Last Kings. "The change of location threw me off."

"Don't worry about it. Do you have my money?"

"Right here," he said and tossed the bag to her feet. "No need to count it. It's all there."

Sadie finished with her nails and placed the file inside of her Birkin crossbody bag. She glanced briskly down at the bag of money and didn't bother to check it. Instead, she stepped around it and walked toward Cam. He couldn't read the expression on her beautiful face, but still he held his ground.

"Unlike you to travel alone," Cam said when she was directly in front of him.

"I didn't think I needed an army to collect a payment," Sadie said, and the corners of her lips twitched. "Carry the bag to my car."

Sadie stepped around him after her instruction and started toward the tunnel entrance. The click-clack of her heels echoed against the walls, and Cam clenched his jaw and fists. Knowing that was her last order to him, he kept his emotions in check and picked up the bag of money. He walked behind her, but not too closely. He stared at the back of her head and waited for the first bullet to strike her body. He held his breath as her right foot hit the sunlight, and then her left. In seconds her body would be riddled with bullets, and her designer suit would be bloody . . . but when she was completely unshielded by the tunnel, nothing happened. Confused, Cam too stepped out of the tunnel and glanced around the construction site. His men had distinct instructions to fire upon sight, but it was quieter than when he had come. In fact . . .

Cam glanced to where he'd left Felix standing next to the running car, but he was nowhere to be seen. He wasn't even in the driver's seat of the vehicle, and the car had been turned off. Cam's brow furrowed. He grabbed his phone from his pocket and dialed Dwayne's number. The phone rang and rang until the automated voicemail picked up. Where was he? And why hadn't he followed instructions? Cam looked up to see Sadie facing him with a smirk on her lips. As she stared, he saw a glimmer of pleasure flash across her face.

"You might as well put that phone away. There's no point," she said. "I was supposed to walk out here and *boom,* off with my head, right?"

"I don't know what you're talking about," Cam told her with a straight face.

"You don't? Then let me enlighten you," she said. "Do you think that I would ever let you run any business or push any of my work without you being watched? Especially after you worked for Khiron when he slid into my city?"

"So, you never trusted me then."

"Correction: I presented you with an opportunity to redeem yourself . . . and you've failed."

The two of them stared into each other's eyes for a few seconds, his filled with thirst and hatred, and hers filled with amusement. In a swift motion, he reached for the Glock on his hip, but she didn't budge. It wasn't until he heard the clicking of a gun cocking behind his head that he understood why.

"I wouldn't do that if I were you," a woman's menacing voice warned. "Not unless you want to join your friends and driver. Hands up."

Cam did as he was told, glaring at Sadie the entire time. It had been a setup. The meeting, the change of location. If what she said was true, he had no idea who the rat was in his camp. She could have known about his plan for weeks.

"I brought you something," the voice behind him said.

She dropped something on his designer shoe, and when he looked down to see what it was, he almost threw up everything in his stomach. It was a severed head, but not just any severed head. *Dwayne.* His eyes were still open, staring blankly up at Cam.

"What the fuck!" he exclaimed and kicked it feverishly away. "You killed Dwayne!"

"And everybody else you brought with you, including your driver. He seemed like a sweet man. Sorry he had to work for a snake like you," the woman behind him said as she nudged the back of his head roughly with her gun.

"Enough, Rhonnie," Sadie instructed.

Cam's blood instantly ran cold. He recognized the name as one of Sadie's two security guards. At first, it was laughable that she trusted two women to protect her with their lives, but after seeing what they were capable of, those same laughs were muffled. Rhonnie and her sister, Ahli, weren't just goons. They were savages. Dwayne's severed head was proof of that.

"I thought you said you didn't bring an army."

"I didn't, but you should know I always keep a few shooters with me," Sadie said, turning her attention back to Cam. "You remind me a lot of Khiron, do you know that? So thirsty for power that you would do anything to get it. I pity you for that."

"Easy for you to say when you have all the power," Cam spat.

"But do you know why I have power? Because I never wanted it. The difference between you and me is that I would have been content working under my cousin, Ray, and breaking bread with my people. People I could trust, because when you have a loyal team, you can eat forever. However, fate dealt a different hand for me. I didn't have to take my throne. It was granted to me."

"All of this to say what?" he spat.

"If you were meant to rule the streets, it would be me with a bullet in my head, and not you."

Cam was in the middle of inhaling one last breath when the trigger was pulled behind his head. He didn't stand a chance with a bullet entering his skull at that close range. Blood and brains exploded everywhere, and his body dropped like a heavy weight next to his soldier's head.

Sadie didn't blink, but she did she turn her nose up in disgust. She glanced down at her suit to make sure not even a droplet of blood had gotten on it and was happy to see that none had. When she glanced back to Rhonnie, she gave her a look and shook her head.

"What?" Rhonnie asked with her hands up. "I thought you wanted me to shoot this nigga."

"I did. That's not what the look is for. I'm talking about that," Sadie said and pointed to the head. "Sadistic much?"

"I thought it would be a nice touch. Something to send the message to anyone out there who is even thinking about crossing The Last Kings." Rhonnie grinned and tucked her gun under the black hoodie she had on.

"If you say so. Were there any survivors?" Sadie asked and opened the front door of her Mercedes.

"No. The four of them didn't even see me coming from where they were hiding behind the equipment. Do you want me to call someone to clean the mess up?"

Sadie stared at Cam's dead body and watched him bleed out for a few moments before shaking her head. "Leave them all here," she said after pondering it. "Let the construction crew find their bodies in the morning. Like you said, this will send a message. As merciful as I've been these past years, I don't need anyone thinking I've lost my touch. The Last Kings isn't going anywhere ever again.

"Let's go. We have an important meeting tomorrow, and I need both you and your sister to be sharp. I allowed you to cover for Ahli today, and luckily you pulled the job off. But tomorrow, I need the two of you by my side. I don't trust anyone else."

"What's so special about tomorrow?" Rhonnie inquired, walking to the passenger's door.

Sadie didn't say anything until the two of them were both inside with the doors shut. She could feel Rhonnie's eyes burning a hole in the side of her cheek, waiting for an answer. Sadie turned to face Rhonnie with a mischievous shimmer in her eyes.

"*Vita E Morte* is ready to be put on the market."

Chapter 2

It wasn't the sound of the television, the birds chirping outside the window, or even the housekeeper who kept knocking on the hotel room door that woke Ahli Malone up. No, her eyes didn't open until her hand reached to the right side of the bed and was met with nothing but air. The white oversized comforter was soft and warm around Ahli's body as she sat up and stretched her arms in the air. Glancing around the hotel suite, she searched for the person responsible for making the night before so exceptional. However, her boyfriend, Brayland, was nowhere to be found. When she looked down to where he had fallen asleep beside her, she saw a folded piece of paper on his pillow. It was a note. She grabbed and unfolded it, trying to fight the smile creeping to her lips.

Last night was the most fun I've had in a while. I don't remember the last time I danced. I wish I could see your face waking up to me, but the boss called me in. I love you.

P.S. Whatever that thing was you did with your tongue? I like it.

A giggle slipped through her lips, and she kissed the note before letting it fall on the bed. She was a little upset that they wouldn't be able to grab breakfast together, but duty called. Ahli knew what that meant. The day before was the first day off either one of them had in six months, and just like that, it was over. Since Brayland had driven and was now gone, she figured she would just call a driver to take her back to the mansion.

Ahli got out of bed and went to the desk her phone was charging on to check for any missed messages or calls. There was nothing on the screen when she looked, but still she decided to shower and get dressed. In her realm of work, it was better to be ready instead of having to get ready when someone summoned her. She unsnapped her bra, letting it and her lace panties fall to the ground as she walked to the large bathroom. She turned the water in the glass-enclosed shower to the hottest that she could stand and got in.

Placing her hands on the wall in front of her, she allowed the water to run from her hair to her toes. Her eyes were closed, and the events from the past three years passed on the backs of her lids. If someone else were to tell her story, Ahli wasn't alive in it. She and her sister, Rhonnie, supposedly died three years ago at the Opulent Inn in the clutches of Madame, the woman originally in search of *Vita E Morte.* Ahli's mother and father had hidden the formula, but Madame never stopped searching. In fact, the risk their parents took cost their father his life. So when Sadie Thomas, a leader of one of the biggest drug cartels in the United States, saved them and killed Madame, it wasn't hard to say goodbye to their lives from before. They were able to fall completely off the grid, although both refused to get new names. Technically, on paper, they didn't exist anymore, but Ahli was all right with that.

After the untimely death of her father, Quinton, and the horrific events that followed, Ahli didn't know what her purpose was anymore. Her mother had died years before that, and Rhonnie was all she had. Ahli was a thief trained in combat with nobody to rob and nobody calling the shots. It wasn't until Sadie rescued them that she found a new purpose, and that was protecting the head of The Last Kings at any cost. Sadie hired both Ahli and Rhonnie to be her personal security detail after seeing what they were capable of, and she gave them a second chance to live.

Ahli stood up straight and finished washing herself before turning off the water. She stepped out of the shower and wrapped one of the white towels around her body. Her long, wet hair hung loosely around her face when she exited the bathroom. She almost jumped out of her body when she saw a woman sitting with her back to her on the hotel bed.

"What the fuck," Ahli breathed when the woman turned her head to face her. "Sadie, you scared the hell out of me."

"We thought to call, but then we figured the element of surprise would be better," Rhonnie's voice sounded, and she rounded the corner from the small kitchen in the suite. "So, surprise!"

Rhonnie held her hands up and wiggled her fingers. She was dressed in a nice tan suit with a blazer and red heels. Her hair was pulled up into a ponytail broadcasting her cheekbones and chin definition. She looked so ridiculous moving her fingers around that Ahli almost laughed, but she was too busy trying to figure out how they'd gotten in her room. Actually, she wanted to know how they even found her.

"Your credit card is attached to my account, remember?" Sadie said, seeing the look of confusion on Ahli's face.

The smile on Sadie's face was kind, and Ahli shook her head sheepishly. For the most part, Sadie gave both women their privacy. So much so that Ahli had forgotten that their entire existence was attached to hers.

"I didn't think you would need us until later today," Ahli said, pulling a black suit and some lotion from her overnight bag, "but Brayland said you called him into work."

"About that." The smile on Sadie's face turned into a serious line. "I sent him on a few runs, just as extra muscle. But honestly, I just needed him out of the way."

"Out of the way for what?"

"I called a meeting for later, and I only want the two of you to attend it with me," Sadie answered. "I want to make sure everything goes smoothly. Nothing like what happened yesterday."

Sadie shot Rhonnie a look that made Ahli look at her too. Rhonnie shrugged her shoulders, but Ahli could tell by the malevolent smirk on her face that she'd done something ridiculous.

"Do I even want to know, NaNa?" Ahli asked with a raised brow, calling her sister by the nickname she'd given her when they were younger.

"I didn't even do too much this time. I just used a machete on one of the dudes rolling with Cam, that's all."

"So you're Madame now?" Ahli asked, making a face as she reflected on Madame's killing methods. "I would have thought that after what happened, you wouldn't want to play with knives."

"Maybe if Sadie hadn't paid for my complete facial and body reconstructive surgery, but now I'm good as new!" Rhonnie ran her hand down the side of her face.

Just by looking at the two of them, a person would never be able to tell that their bodies had once been covered in several cuts and gashes. They had to undergo a few surgeries, but in the end, there wasn't even a blemish that stood out. Ahli just rolled her eyes at her sister and let the towel drop to the ground, not caring that she was standing there naked.

"It sounds like this is an important meeting," she pondered aloud as she applied lotion to her body. "And if it's so important, why are Rhonnie and I the only security detail you want to have? Usually you roll a few trucks deep to important things."

"This is so important that I only want the two I trust the most with me," Sadie said while she and Rhonnie exchanged a look.

"And why is that?"

"*Vita E Morte* is ready to be placed on the market," Rhonnie answered.

Ahli stopped rubbing lotion on her leg mid-stroke. "W . . . what?" Ahli's eyes were wide as she looked from Rhonnie to Sadie. "I didn't think it would be ready so soon."

"So soon?" Sadie asked, furrowing her brow. "My scientists in the lab in Azua have been working day and night for the past three years to perfect the drug. It's finally ready. I'll be presenting it to potential buyers today."

"Are you sure it's the right time?" Ahli asked, getting dressed into her form-fitting suit. "I mean, I thought business has been doing well."

"If there's one thing you should know about me by now, it's that there is never such a thing as too much money," Sadie told her and eyed her suspiciously. "Are you good, Ahli? You can be honest with me about whatever you're feeling."

"Yeah, I just . . . I guess I never thought of how I would really feel when *Vita E Morte* was ready. I mean, my mother hid it for a reason. I can't help but to think, what if she was right? Maybe it isn't supposed to be on the streets."

"Shit, crack wasn't supposed to be on the streets. But you see fiends buying eight balls left and right," Rhonnie butted in. "I'm with Sadie on this one, sister. I mean, this is going to be big. Probably bigger than the crack epidemic, and it's *ours.* And Mom had a whole life that we never knew about. How do we know what her real reasons were for hiding the formula?"

Ahli chose to be quiet because to that she didn't have a rebuttal. She finished getting dressed and went back into the bathroom to brush her teeth and pull her hair up into a bun. Her thoughts were all over the place. Just an hour ago, she had been in pure bliss, but now she had an uneasy feeling in the pit of her stomach. However, she had to remember that it had been *she* who told Sadie where to find the formula, and it had been *she* who gave Sadie the okay to use it. Ahli sighed in the mirror and rubbed her hands over her small waist. She hoped that she wouldn't have to ruin another work suit at the meeting later. She'd just replaced an entire closetful.

"You all right in here?" Sadie appeared in the doorway.

"I'm just finishing up," Ahli said a little more tersely than she meant to, and it didn't go unnoticed by Sadie.

"If you want me to get someone else to come, that's all right. But I did want to tell you face-to-face what the meeting was about."

"No, it's fine. I'll go."

"Are you sure?"

"Yes." Ahli nodded and she meant it. "You saved our lives, and for that I owe you my service and allegiance. Where you go, I go."

"That's what I like to hear," Sadie said and smiled. "And speaking of what I like to hear, how was your night off?"

"It was amazing," Ahli said as a happy feeling came over her. "We went to dinner at Eddie V's, and then he surprised me by taking me to Amor to go dancing. It's been so long since I felt that free. It was like time stopped for a few hours. And as you see, we ended up here for the night. But now I'm thinking that I should have been with you two. What happened to Cam?"

"The same thing that happens to everyone who goes against the family," Sadie said dryly. "His body was found at a construction site. It's been a while since somebody moved on us in a way like that, and hopefully this situation with Cam is a reminder not to. Now hurry up and finish getting ready. I have something that you and your sister are going to like."

"New guns?" Ahli guessed, and her eyes lit up.

"New guns," Sadie confirmed with a wink.

That was all she needed to say for Ahli to put pep in her step. She was satisfied with the silicon carbide–grip Glock 19 pistols she had, but she wouldn't turn down any new weapons. Getting new firearms was like getting new toys for her and Rhonnie. Within minutes, she had everything she came with thrown in her overnight bag, ready to go. They left the hotel and traveled to Sadie's mansion in Rhonnie's snow white Rolls-Royce.

Rhonnie and Ahli had moved in with Sadie when they were relocated to Detroit. Sadie's $2 million home had been built on land that she purchased, complete with a small pond and forest area in the backyard where the girls trained. The twenty-acre property was beautiful and desolate, just the way she liked it.

The gate surrounding the property opened when they got to it, and Rhonnie drove through. She took the Rolls-Royce into the garage attached to the mansion. The garage was the size of a house itself, being as it held all twelve of their vehicles. When they all were out of the car, Sadie led the way.

"They're in the shooting range," Sadie said over her shoulder, taking them inside the house.

They followed her down one of many long hallways to an elevator at the end of it. Besides elevators, another one of the modifications Sadie had made to the home was having a gun range built inside of it, enclosed by soundproof walls, complete with bulletproof glass and unlimited firepower. It was Ahli's favorite place to go when she needed to let off some steam.

"I had Alberto bring this shipment directly to the house because I put this order together meticulously for you two," Sadie said once they stepped out of the elevator and into the bottom level of the house.

The lights in the wide hallway were motion-sensor operated, and with each step, a new area lit up. Every wall was white, and the floor was marble with black-and-white furniture. They walked past the spa room, the theater, and Sadie's office before they came to the gun range. Unable to hold her excitement in, Rhonnie hurried past them and was the first to enter.

"Goddamn, Sadie," Ahli heard her sister say in an amazed tone.

Curious, Ahli quickly stepped around her boss and went to see what Rhonnie was talking about. As soon as she entered the bright room, she went directly to the artillery station on her left. A table had been laid out, and the top of it was covered with weapons and ammunition. Rhonnie was already standing in front of it, holding what looked to be an assault rifle, an AKM to be exact. That wasn't all that was there. Ahli's eyes went to two fully loaded M16 and M4 carbine tactical rifles, complete with scopes and drum mags. Next to those were four brand new Glocks 19 pistols with black frames and diamond-encrusted slides. Lastly, she took notice of the AR-15 rifles, and although her fingers were itching to shoot one, she grabbed an M4 instead. Even with all the customizations, it was still lightweight in her grip. When she saw that it had all the functionality for a soldier to use, she raised her brow at Sadie.

"Are these military grade?"

"Yes. I had them made to order. No serial numbers or any other identifiers."

"Ghost guns."

"Ghost guns," Sadie confirmed.

"I like this," Rhonnie said, putting the AKM back and grabbing an AR-15. "This AR has a carbon-fiber barrel."

"I thought you would prefer it over a bull barrel," Sadie told her. "But if you need one, I ordered some of those, too."

"Cool," Rhonnie said and went back to examining all the guns.

Ahli placed the M4 down and turned her attention to Sadie. She couldn't wait to shoot with her new toys, but there was something itching at her in the back of her mind. "Why do we need military-grade weapons?"

"In light of this new drug, I want to take every precaution possible to avoid any chaos when it hits the streets. And if it inevitably breaks out anyway, I expect you two to contain it."

Her answer was simple, and Rhonnie nodded. However, Ahli read between the lines. Sadie might have been her boss, but she was also the only friend she'd ever had besides her sister. She was able to read Sadie the same way she could Rhonnie, and she always knew when something wasn't right.

"You're worried."

"I didn't say that," Sadie countered, grabbing one of the Glocks and heading over to the first shooting station.

"Then why are you expecting chaos?"

"Sometimes the world reacts to change in a good way and sometimes it doesn't. *Vita E Morte* is something no other kingpin has, and it's something they won't ever be able to obtain . . . without me. I'm the only one with the formula, and when the market for it opens, some might not want to go through me to get it. And, well, you know what might happen after that."

"So you *are* worried."

"No," Sadie said, aiming the gun at the paper target and emptying the clip. After the last shot rang, she turned back to Ahli and handed her the weapon. "Because I just bought you new guns, and I know you'll use them well. Those, by the way, are just the ones that would fit on the table. You two have a few hours. Have some fun. But I need you dressed and ready by four o'clock sharp. There will be a driver here to pick us up."

Ahli watched her walk out of the room without another word. She almost called after her but stopped herself when she realized that she didn't have anything else to say. The only thing that she could do was trust her boss like she'd done for the past three years. In the time she'd worked for Sadie, she learned quickly that her boss was a master of covering all her bases even when she didn't need to. It was what made her so elite at what she did. However, there was something different about her honesty that time. It was the kind of different that Ahli couldn't put her finger on.

Instead of trying to, she grabbed a pair of earmuffs and a firearm. Taking her place in the first shooting stall where Sadie had been, she noticed that the paper target had received all head shots.

Chapter 3

A small smile was frozen on Sadie's lips as she made her way to her master suite inside of the mansion. She had been waiting for this day for a long time, and it had finally come. It was no secret that money had always been her motivation, ever since her cousin Ray had put her on in the game all those years ago. But now she would have something to set her apart from every other hustler in the world.

Quiet as kept, *Vita E Morte* had been the only thing keeping her going for the last six months, not just because she was dedicated and driven to put it out, but because it had saved her from becoming a victim to her own emotions. There were a few things that she couldn't afford to think about when so much was on the line, like her ex-boyfriend, Tyler, and his new fiancée. Because if she thought about it, she would have to come to terms with the fact that he wasn't hers anymore. If she thought about it, she would be forced to admit to herself that she was heartbroken, and that was a feeling she couldn't afford to feel. Not on the brink of her success. Still, a year ago, when she told Tyler she needed a break, she didn't think six months later he would be engaged. She didn't think he would move on so fast. She thought he would wait for her because he loved her. But she was wrong. He had fallen in love with someone else.

As Ray's right-hand man, Tyler was still part of The Last Kings, so she had no choice but to occasionally be around him on a business note. In truth, he had tried a few times to talk to her about where they stood, but she just couldn't. He had made the conscious decision to give another woman his heart, and she had nothing to say to him. Sadie found that if she kept herself busy, she wouldn't think about Tyler. But right then, when she walked into her room and sat on her bed, the only person she wanted to talk to was him.

He knew all about Rhonnie and Ahli and the events that had led her to them. However, she hadn't told anyone but Ray and their team of scientists about the drug. Maybe if Tyler knew the reason she had been so aloof back then, things would have been different. She had been so wrapped up in doing something that hadn't been done in years that the last thing on her mind was a relationship. If she could go back and do things differently, she might have. But she was fashioning a new drug, not a time machine.

Before she knew it, Sadie was on her feet again and inside of her closet. It was vast and mimicked a dressing room in a luxury clothing store. In the very back, there was a jewelry cabinet that held some of her most prized possessions. The entire cabinet was a mirror, and the front of it was outlined with diamonds. As she walked toward it, she stripped herself of her clothing. She looked her curvy body up and down, taking in her reflection as a whole. Gone was the girl who had begged her cousin for a piece of his pie. She had been replaced with a woman who had the spirit of a boss. A boss who would do whatever it took to never fall from grace again.

She opened the door of the cabinet and was standing face-to-face with $2 million worth of jewelry. She reached past all the diamonds and gold and pulled something from the back of the cabinet: a picture. Her face was emotionless as she stared down at the man and woman in the photo. The man was Tyler, and the woman was her. She was holding the camera and had caught the perfect photo of them smiling big under the shining moon. They were sitting on a gondola gliding along the canals of Venice, Italy. Sadie felt her heart tug slightly when she thought back to how Tyler had surprised her with a trip out of the country for a few days. She was so happy, and she would have been content anywhere in the world as long as she was with him.

"I'm going to keep this photo forever."

That was what she had said, and she meant it at the time. But it seemed that their forever had come and gone. A single tear rolled down her cheek and fell on her happy face in the photo. Her chest felt like it had caved in, like someone had knocked all the wind out of her, and she realized she had been holding her breath. When she finally tried to breathe, she was comparable to a fish out of water, gasping at the air. It seemed as if the walls inside the closet were closing in on her, and before more tears could fall, she clenched her eyes shut. She didn't open them until she had regained her wits, and when she did, Sadie forcefully ripped the photo in half before letting the two pieces fall to the floor. She closed the cabinet and left the closet, grabbing the suit and shoes she was going to be wearing on her way out.

She couldn't hear the guns going off in the basement, but Sadie knew Ahli and Rhonnie were down there having a field day. She hadn't expected Rhonnie to have many questions about the meeting, Ahli was the one she had been worried about. Although Ahli was the one who had given the location to the drug's recipe, Sadie figured she hadn't given much thought to the fact that one day it would really be on the market. If Ahli *did* feel any kind of way, she would have to get over it quick. Money was the motive, and there were millions, potentially billions, at their fingertips.

Sadie set the clothes on her California king and went to the bathroom connected to her bedroom. It was one of her favorite parts of the entire house, and she had it designed to fit all her needs. She felt the familiarity of the floor-to-ceiling pebbles underneath her feet as she made her way past the walk-in soaking tub. It was big enough to fit five people, and even though she would have loved to sit and relax, she didn't have the time. So instead, she opted for a steaming hot shower. She turned the knob so that the water inside the glass walls of the shower spouted out and instantly hit her from all sides. She thought that the sting of water would bring her back to the present instead of in and out of her memories of Tyler, but she was wrong.

"I love you, Sadie," she heard and saw his lips say in her mind.

"Stop it," she whispered with her head down and water sliding down her face.

"There's nobody else out there for me."

"Please stop . . ."

"Why are you doing this?"

"Get out of my head!"

The truth was that she was inside her own head. Sadie fell to the floor of the shower and curled up in a ball as she finally let out the grief she'd been holding in. All of the strength she was used to carrying around all the time left her body. She cried loudly, not caring, because no one could hear her anyway. Her sobs were so powerful that her entire body shook, and she shook her head left and right.

"You don't love me," she said out loud to the Tyler in her head. "You moved on. I asked for space to focus on business, *our* business, and you left me! I hate you!"

In that moment, she was reminded that she was still human, and it humbled her deeply. She wasn't just some ruthless hustler. At the end of the day, she was a woman—a woman who had loved and lost her soulmate. She cried and lashed out, banging the glass walls. When there were no more tears in her eyes, she let the shower water replace them.

When Sadie finally got back up, she felt better—not much, but a little bit would do. She cleaned herself and got out of the shower, not realizing exactly how much time had really passed during her episode. When she was dried off, Sadie went back into her bedroom, and she saw that the clock read three o'clock. Although the meeting was at five, she felt rushed because she still needed to get dressed, and the ride there would eat up forty-five minutes of those two hours.

The first thing she did after moisturizing was put her hair into two neat Cherokee braids. Next, she got dressed in her high-waisted maroon skinny pantsuit. She paired that with a black cotton camisole that she tucked into her pants and a black and gold Gucci belt to go around her waist. After sliding into her blazer jacket and pumps, she grabbed a small black Gucci clutch and a white binder off one of the dressers in her room.

Before leaving her suite, she glanced in the mirror at her reflection to make sure there was no trace of the fact that she'd been bawling. Her eyes were a little red, but that was nothing some eye drops couldn't fix. Other than that, her secret was safe with her. Sadie dug in her clutch until her fingers wrapped around the small eye drop bottle, and she applied two drops to each eye.

By the time she got downstairs to the foyer of the mansion, Rhonnie and Ahli were already there waiting in their normal black attire. To the untrained eye, they just looked like two put-together businesswomen, but Sadie could see the small bulge of the guns on their hips.

"Our driver just pulled up," Rhonnie announced, glancing through the glass windows beside the front door. "Are you ready?"

"Beyond," Sadie replied, and the smile that found her lips was genuine.

"Then we should be heading out. After you, boss," Ahli said, opening the door for Sadie to walk through.

Sadie avoided eye contact with her when she did. She didn't understand it, but somehow Ahli always seemed to be able to guess when something was amiss with her. The only people able to do that without trying were Sadie's former best friend, Mocha, and Ray. In truth, Sadie had tried to keep the relationship with both sisters strictly professional. The original plan had been to hire them as security, and that was it. But without anticipating it, the girls had built a tight bond over the years. They were a family now, and the truth was that Sadie would risk her life to save them just as quickly as they would her.

Monroe, their driver, was standing outside of the CEO SUV and holding the back door open for them. He had been Sadie's driver ever since her old driver, Pierre, retired. Monroe was a sweet older man who reminded her a lot of her late grandmother, Rae, just in the male form. He was originally from Oakland, California, and still had the accent. He didn't just drive her around. Sometimes she would have to hear his mouth, too. Back in his day, he had been "the man" in Cali, that was until he relocated to Detroit and settled down with the love of his life. He always had new pointers or told her where she needed to tighten up, and for the most part, she listened. The hair on his head was fully gray, but he was as fit and muscular as a man half his age. Sadie liked for everyone around her to look like money, so he stood before her in a Tom Ford tuxedo with diamond cuff links.

"You look like you should be getting chauffeured instead of driving me around," Sadie teased when she was in earshot.

"You better quit," he said with a big smile. "And for the record, if you didn't pay me so good for driving you around, I wouldn't be able to afford this damn suit."

"Well, for the record, I pay you so well because of the guidance you give me. Not for driving me around," Sadie told him and kissed his cheek.

She got in first and made herself comfortable in the leather seat with her clutch and the white binder in her lap. Rhonnie got in and sat across from her while Ahli sat to her right. When Monroe shut the door and got in himself, they pulled away from the mansion en route to their destination. Sadie had arranged for everyone invited to the meeting to have transportation that would bring them to an undisclosed location. The drive was a good forty-five minutes with traffic, but they arrived in a timely manner.

"The meeting is at the stash house?" Rhonnie made a face when she saw the driveway they were pulling into. They were outside of what looked to be an old, abandoned house, but they all knew it was much more. "I guess there is no better place to hold a meeting of this magnitude than in your own territory."

"Exactly," Sadie said and took notice of the Mercedes SUV parked up the street. "They're here. Come on."

Monroe got the door for them and waited for them to go around the back of the gated house before he got back into the car. When they reached the back door, Rhonnie knocked three times, and it opened. They were met by a tall, handsome man holding an AK-47. When he saw them, the hard look he'd been wearing quickly faded, and when his eyes fell on Ahli, he smiled.

"Brayland? What are you doing here?" Ahli asked.

"Yeah, what *are* you doing here?" Sadie asked with a raised brow because she had sent him to do other things. "I thought I told you to do drops with Gerron and his team."

"I did," Brayland said, stepping back and letting them enter. "This was one of the last stops we had to make. We cleared this spot out to move the work around. But when I saw that truck pull up, I thought I'd stay awhile. Figured you three would pop up soon."

"Nosy ass," Rhonnie said, shaking her head.

"Never that. I just like to be in the know."

"Aka nosy as hell," Rhonnie reiterated.

"Yeah, whatever," Brayland dismissed what she said and turned back to Sadie. "Your people are down there waiting on you."

"Thank you," she said, turning the corner and heading down the dimly lit stairs.

With each step she took, the voices coming from the large basement space grew louder and more distinguishable. She could hear the tension in all of their voices, and she was sure it had something to do with how she had them transported.

"Were the bags over our heads really necessary? You would think she doesn't know a nigga or something," a deep voice commented.

It was a voice that brought joy to her heart, and it had been too long since she'd heard it. When she took the final step off the stairs and into the light, she passed two more of her men holding automatic weapons and peering at their guests with "I wish you would" eyes.

"Thank you, Keith and Lamont, for bringing our guests here unscathed," Sadie said to them before heading for a large, round table in the middle of the dirty carpeted floor.

There were four people sitting around it a few seats apart. The table had a projector in the center of it, as well as a laptop beside it. All four faces were ones she recognized instantly, and her pearly whites flashed when she stepped into the light. Upon seeing her arrive, their tension instantly went away, especially since she greeted them in good spirits.

"Yes, it *was* necessary for my men to bring you here with bags over your heads, Legacy," she said, grinning from ear to ear as she approached them. "Trust or not, some locations I would prefer to remain a secret, sorry. Sorry about having them take your guns, too."

"Sadie!" Legacy said, standing and pulling her into a deep embrace. "It's been too long."

"That it has," Sadie said when she pulled away to get a good look at him. "Did you get bigger? I don't remember you being this tall."

"Shit, the way you've been ghost, I'm surprised you even remember me at all. No calls, no texts. Shit, I didn't even have your new number until you hit me up the other day," he said in a joking manner, but Sadie knew he was serious by the hurt look in his eyes.

He had a right to be hurt by her absence. After all, there was once a time when the two of them had been as close as siblings. When Khiron had almost defeated her, Legacy was the one who was in her corner. He was the ally who loaned his own army just so she could get her city back. If it weren't for Legacy, she wouldn't be standing there in front of him as one of the highest-ranking bosses in the States. He had saved not only her, but The Last Kings. However, even with that being said, Sadie felt like she had earned the right to keep to herself for a while. They were both doing their own things. Still, she hadn't meant to be out of reach for five months.

"I've just been getting some shit in order, that's all," she said simply, but by the way he looked at her, she knew it wasn't a good enough answer.

"We'll talk, but for now, how about you introduce me to these lovely ladies behind you," Legacy said, motioning to Rhonnie and Ahli, who had followed Sadie down the stairs.

"Trust me, those two are anything but ladies," said the person in the seat next to Legacy.

The voice belonged to Arrik, one of Sadie's underbosses who had expanded The Last Kings' reach to Omaha, Nebraska. His long hair was braided Iverson style, and he was dressed the most casual out of everyone at the table. Arrik knew Rhonnie and Ahli too well, being as they were the ones who robbed him three years prior. If it hadn't been for that greedy hit, Sadie would have never been led to them. It was a bad that ended in good, but Arrik still held a small grudge. See, he ran an airtight camp, so for them to have been able to pull off something like that spoke volumes of their skillset. Seeing them was a forever reminder of the time he was caught lacking.

"Hater," Rhonnie directed to him. "You know you love us."

"Humph. Sike, nigga," Arrik scoffed.

"These two are my security," Sadie answered Legacy's question, setting the binder and her clutch down on the table.

"That's my sister, Ahli, and I'm Rhonnie," Rhonnie said, raising her right hand for a handshake. "And I heard your name is Legacy, but I think I'm just gon' call you Fine, because you're fine as hell! Goddamn, Sadie! I thought this was a business meeting, not a tryout for the sexiest motherfuckas in the world."

"It's not. And I'm married, so call me Legacy," Legacy said, shaking her right hand with his left and flashing the ring on his finger. He turned to Sadie and raised a brow. "You sure this is who you can trust with your safety?"

"Trust me, she has me covered," Sadie told him, but she didn't miss an opportunity to shoot Rhonnie a look that said to settle down.

Rhonnie and Ahli took their seats at the table, and Legacy did the same, making sure he was far away from Rhonnie. Sadie focused her attention on the other two men sitting at the table. They hadn't said a word, and instead were observing the scene. The older one was known as King Dex. He, too, was a kingpin in Nebraska, but the two of them had agreed to coexist peacefully. He not only had a work ethic that she admired, but his love for the hustle was vintage. He ran his business out of sight the same way she did, and that was something Sadie respected. She had placed the offer on the table for King Dex to join The Last Kings, but he respectfully declined at that time. This go-around, Sadie thought it would be different. Especially since no one who *wasn't* a Last King would have access to *Vita E Morte*.

Next to King Dex was a young man who had gotten Sadie's attention within the past year. She'd been keeping tabs on him after the death of his older brother, Cane Anderson. See, Cane didn't just have love in his city, he was all around the world with it. Sadie had put some money in his pockets by hiring him to put in some work for her after they met. He was a good kid who grew to be an even better man. She heard that L.A. wept when he passed, and she regretted not being able to make the funeral. It was rumored that L.A.'s kingpin, Dubb, had something to do with Cane's death, and soon after the funeral, he was dead too. The story was what piqued her interest, but Cane's little brother, Cyril, was what kept it.

He didn't know it, but he had the eyes of the biggest drug operation on him the moment he accepted the role of L.A.'s new kingpin. At first, she had plans to send Rhonnie in to exterminate him so that they could move in on L.A.'s territories, because what did a kid like him know about being the head of a major operation? But then she remembered she was his age when they started The Last Kings. Instead of killing him, she decided to give him a chance.

She watched him closely and saw him come into himself. In a year's time, Cyril became five times the boss of what Sadie expected him to be. He moved work faster than anyone she'd ever seen, and his operation was solid. What she liked most about him was that he was smart and he didn't make decisions based on emotion. All of his moves were calculated, and that was why she approached him with her offer. Unlike King Dex, Cyril welcomed the opportunity of being part of a bigger family. Instead of needing a connect, he now *was* the connect for L.A., and Sadie was able to expand without another murder on her hands. Needless to say, when she called and told him about a new business opportunity, he was right there.

"What's up, Sadie." He nodded at her.

"I'm glad you could make it, Cyril. You too, King Dex."

"I'm just hoping it was worth the trip," King Dex said in a dull tone. "I hope you're not trying to talk me into joining The Last Kings again."

"Actually, I'm not," Sadie said, smirking at him. "But by the time I'm done talking, you'll be begging for a throne to sit on."

"Is that right?"

"That's right," she confirmed. "Everybody get comfortable and pay close attention to what I'm about to say."

Out of the corner of her eye, she saw movement by the stairs. When she looked, she realized that it was just Brayland switching positions with the soldiers who had been manning the basement. It was apparent that he really didn't want to miss what was going on down there. Sadie didn't care. She knew Ahli was just going to tell him everything later anyway. She powered on the two devices on the table and grabbed the wireless mouse for the laptop. She then directed everyone's attention to the wall the projector was shooting on. She'd put together a slideshow for them all to view, and the first slide was three words in big, slanted letters. Walking to the wall, she used her finger to point while looking at them all.

"'*Vita E Morte,*'" Sadie read aloud. "The future of The Last Kings."

"*Vita E Morte?*" Arrik asked, making a confused face. "That sounds like a TV show or some shit. What the fuck is that?"

"I'm glad you asked, and so nicely, too," Sadie said sarcastically before continuing. "Some people believe that drugs poison the world, and in a sense, they do. But we can't ignore the fact that they often help more than they hurt. It all comes down to the user. The problem lies in the quantity of intake. The need."

"But isn't the need what brings the customer back?" King Dex asked.

"This is true, but we can't ignore the danger of the large quantities people choose to indulge in, nor can we ignore the fake dealers who sell drugs equivalent to toxic waste."

"So you want us, the drug dealers, to sympathize with the fiends?" Arrik asked, raising a brow.

"No, that's not what I'm asking at all," Sadie said, shaking her head with the hint of a smirk on her lips. "Arrik, do you know the one drug *everyone* always comes back to because it's safe?"

"Shit, weed?"

"Ding ding! You are correct. Marijuana is the right answer. But the problem with weed is that the high wears off fast. And that's why people search for a higher and longer-lasting high. There is a reason why it is called a gateway drug."

"But gateway drugs have always been good for the comeback clientele," Cyril pitched in.

"But are they really? The drugs inside those gates may have a stronger high, but they're not long-lasting either.

So they indulge in things like cocaine, heroin, and meth in large quantities," Sadie stated and clicked the mouse in her hand to go to the next slide, which was a page filled completely with names in small font. "As you know, The Last Kings keeps a tally of their most prominent clients. What you're looking at right now is a list of deceased clients around the country who died from an overdose in the past year. Almost two hundred names are on this list."

"Two hundred?" Legacy chuckled, looking from the slide back to Sadie. "That list isn't nearly as big as the list of living clients. Not only that, but with all of the expansions, especially Los Angeles, we can easily replace the ones we've lost, and fast."

"True, but *how* fast can we do that? And who's to say more won't die off in that time?" Sadie asked and went to the next slide. "I took the liberty of calculating what each one of those names spent on our product alone in two years, and I came up with this number."

"Ten million dollars," Ahli read aloud.

"Roughly," Sadie said. "I'm very wealthy, and even to me that number seems alarming. At the rate the economy is going, with the heightening of depression and anxiety in this country, I can see that number doubling in a year's time. People are killing themselves with the high that's supposed to make them feel better. Yeah, like you said, Legacy, we can expand even more to make up for what we've lost. But even doing that, there are startup costs for a new location, hiring people I can trust to run the operation, *and* distribution."

"So, what are you saying?" Arrik asked. "I'm sure you didn't have me travel all the way here from Nebraska to tell me two hundred people died this year for being greedy with their high."

"You're very right." Sadie nodded. "I understand that we are just the dealers and that, once the drugs are out of our hands, what the user decides to do with them is on them. I also understand that there is nothing I can do to prevent someone from overdosing if they choose to intake a high quantity of drugs. We've already said that weed is the one drug everyone goes back to. Can anybody tell me why?"

"Because you may be a little sluggish or hungry, but you're still you," Cyril answered when everyone else failed to. "Coke, pills, and all that other shit changes you, and I think people know that. So they go back to weed, but—"

"The high wears off fast, putting them back in the same boat," Sadie finished for him. "But what would you all say if I told you that I have a solution to that?"

"And that solution is this . . . *Vita* stuff?" King Dex asked as if the thought amused him. "You say that as if you've made a new drug."

"Yes, that's exactly what I'm saying," Sadie said.

The smile on her lips spread slowly as she watched all of them, even Ahli and Rhonnie, sit up in their seats. Sadie let her words loom over the room for a few moments before she clicked the next slide. A photo of a small white pill popped up, and engraved in it were the letters "VEM." She let them look at it for a few seconds before she clicked to the next slide, which was a five-minute video. The video had been taken inside the labs in Azua and showed the effects of what taking one VEM had on five different patients over the course of a week. They watched them complete normal day-to-day tasks and talk about how they felt while on the drug. One of the patients, a black woman in her mid-thirties, appeared on camera with a bright smile on her face. She was sitting on a chair in the middle of what looked to be a bedroom in the lab.

"How did you feel?" an off-screen voice asked her soothingly.

"I felt . . . fantastic," she told him. "It's crazy. I took one pill, and five minutes later, it was like I smoked a fat blunt of Granddaddy Purp, except I didn't come down from the high after a few hours."

"And when did you come down from that high?"

"This morning."

"And when did you take the pill?"

"I think two days ago."

"Did you have a headache when the high wore off?"

"No. It was just like my feet touched back down on the ground. I can't . . . I can't explain the feeling the pill gave me. I just felt good, really good. Like I could do anything. After that, I don't know if smoking a blunt will ever be good enough, and the relaxing high other pills used to give me just seem mediocre now. This is just . . . it's crazy. Can I . . . can I have another? Another pill, I mean."

"We have just a few more questions to get through, and then yes. Yes, you can."

The video suddenly cut to another patient. That time it was a white man in his early twenties. He, too, was sitting in a chair facing the camera, talking to someone off-screen. He was wearing a short-sleeved shirt, and the needle markings on his arms stuck out like a sore thumb.

"I've never felt like that in my life. It was like I was outside of my body, watching myself live my life," he was saying. "Except I wasn't fucking shit up like I usually do when I'm high on coke and heroin. I was high for two days, and in those two days, I was more productive in this room than I have been anywhere else in years."

"Explain?" the off-camera voice asked.

"I mean, I cleaned it, for one, and I never clean shit. I let my wife do that. That's one of the reasons she hates me. I'm always high, dirtying up shit, breaking things, and angry."

The man suddenly looked puzzled as if he had just realized something.

"Is something wrong?" the off-camera voice asked.

"Yeah. I mean, no." The white man shook his head. "I just thought of something. I've been angry at the world for the past three years since my mom died. Not a day has gone by that I wasn't angry . . . until I took that pill you gave me. I'm not even angry now, and the high is gone. Did I tell you I started writing poetry in that notebook you gave all of us to document shit in?"

"Really?"

"Yeah, man, and I didn't even know I could write poetry. I didn't know I could not be angry all the time. When I was high, I just felt like . . ."

"Like what?"

"Like I could do anything."

"If I told you right now that in order to get another pill you would have to throw away the needles and heroin you don't think we know you snuck in here, what would you do?"

Without hesitation, the white man on the video stood up and went to the twin-sized bed behind him. He reached under the pillow and pulled the needles and drugs out, tossed them into the waste bin by the bed, and handed the bin to the person off camera.

"Can I have another pill now?"

Sadie froze the camera on the man's eager, almost-desperate face. She wanted the people in the room to see the need for VEM, and by the intrigued looks on their faces, they did. Before she spoke again, she grabbed the thick white binder that she'd brought with her and opened it. Inside, stapled to the paper in the binder, were four Baggies that each contained 500 pills. She tore the Baggies from the binder and went around the table, placing them in front of Legacy, Arrik, King Dex, and Cyril.

"VEM comes in the form of a single pill, and as you can see, the subjects used for testing are all different races and sizes," Sadie started. "As you can also see, they had better than great reactions to the drug. Not only does it give you a high comparable to the best weed you've ever smoked, but it has no side effects. One pill lasts up to two days, guaranteed, and it doesn't leave the user stuck or too high like crack, cocaine, or heroin. While high on VEM, you are still more than capable of doing all of your daily tasks while feeling good and confident about yourself. No red eyes, munchies, or feeling sluggish. Just a natural cloud-nine high for two days straight. Also, did I mention that it is undetectable in any existing drug-testing process used in the world?"

"So, we're supposed to believe the words of five users in a video?"

"No, but you can believe the hundreds of users already hooked in Azua," Sadie said, clicking to the next slide.

Suddenly they were all watching videos of loud clubs filled with people partying and popping VEM. Many of the club-goers were holding the small Baggies with white pills in their hands. The next slides were photos of restaurants and even schools that had people casually popping the pills from the small Baggies, all smiles.

Sadie watched Ahli's expression of wonder shift to one of indifference. Sadie hadn't told her that they had already started selling it overseas. She knew now, though.

"And so you all don't feel like guinea pigs, I want to let you know I'm starting distribution here in Michigan tomorrow," Sadie informed them all.

"Tomorrow?" Ahli asked, clearly taken aback.

"Yes, tomorrow, and I'm going to need you and Rhonnie to plug all my lieutenants."

Ahli looked like she wanted to say something else, but her sister nudged her.

"We'll be on it," Rhonnie said with a nod.

"How much does a single pill go for?" King Dex asked.

"One two-milligram tablet is one hundred dollars," Sadie answered.

"So ten of them is a rack," Cyril said, doing the math. "Damn."

"How did you come up with the recipe for this drug?" King Dex asked with a raised brow. "Forgive me for asking, but it seems like you've done something that nobody else has done since the crack era. I'm just trying to figure out how."

"Let's just say a little birdie pointed me in the right direction," Sadie answered simply. "*Vita E Morte* is and will always be something that only The Last Kings will have. Even if, and I say this loosely, you were to get robbed of your entire supply, the drug will never be able to be duplicated. If you were to try to figure out on your own how to make it, you wouldn't be able to. Not without the best team of scientists in the world, and I already hired them. And since nobody at this table has more money than me, you'll never be able to buy them out."

"Ooooh, big flex," Arrik said, shaking the bag of pills. "So what do you want us to do? Buy these off you?"

"No. Consider them a gift from me. Those are yours to distribute. I want you to see firsthand the treasure I have given you. I have confidence that I will be hearing from each of you soon. Very soon." Sadie connected eyes with King Dex. "Those are on me, but when you want to buy, and I'm sure you'll want to, the only way to do so is to merge."

"If what you're saying about this drug is true, we will cross that bridge when we get there," King Dex said without batting an eye.

"Fair enough," Sadie told him respectfully. "Now, gentlemen, this meeting is adjourned. Unfortunately, it's time for the bags to go back over your heads so you can leave this place and go back to your car."

She nodded to Brayland, who already had four cloth bags in his hands. Nobody except Legacy put up a fuss when the bag went over their head, but it was what it was. Sadie was different. Losing the two people she loved most in the world had changed her. The goons who had brought the four men there came back down to the basement and led them out of the stash house.

When it was their turn to leave, Rhonnie and Ahli went up the stairs first. As Ahli passed where Brayland was standing, he grabbed her hand. Sadie was a little ways behind them, but she was close enough to hear the exchange.

"Was that what I thought it was?" Brayland asked, and Ahli pulled her hand away from him.

"Not now," was her response, and she continued up the stairs.

Brayland's eyes went from the back of Ahli's head to Sadie. The look he gave her was indifferent, as if he were trying to figure out exactly who she was. Sadie didn't blame him. The old Sadie might have considered him like a little brother. In fact, he had lived in her home for a while when he first got to Detroit. But the fact remained that the ones who had been the closest to her barely knew her anymore, and she knew it was because she pushed them away. The only thing on her mind was taking the game by storm . . . again.

Chapter 4

Ding-dong!

The doorbell ringing caught Sadie off guard. She wasn't expecting company, especially not that late. She and the girls had just gotten back home from their meeting, and she was about to turn in after having a glass of D'Usse. Rhonnie and Ahli were all the way on their side of the house, and the security around the mansion was supposed to make sure nobody who wasn't invited ever got to the front door.

At the time the bell rang, Sadie had been pouring what was left in her glass of alcohol down the sink in the kitchen's center island. Before going to see who was at her house, she reached under the marble island top and pulled a Beretta from its concealment plate. The foyer was dark as she walked to the front door and cocked the gun. She peered through the peephole.

"I should have known," she sighed when she saw who it was. Swinging the door open, she let the hand holding the gun fall to her side while she put her other hand on her hip. "How did you find me, Legacy?"

He took one look at the weapon in her hand and grinned. "Easy." He shrugged in his suit. "I called Ray. Now, are you going to invite me in or what?"

Sadie glared at him briefly before stepping aside so he could step inside. "I was in the kitchen," she said, gesturing with the gun for him to follow her.

"Nice place," he said, looking around when they got to their destination. "I bet it looks even better during the daytime."

"It does," Sadie said tersely and put her weapon back where she got it from. "Now, do you care to tell me why you're popping up at my house instead of on your way back to Miami?"

Legacy didn't answer. In fact, he downright ignored her. He grabbed the bottle of D'Usse and walked to her cabinet of glasses like he owned the place. After grabbing one and getting some ice from the freezer, he poured himself a glass and sat down on a stool by the island.

Sadie stared at him with disbelief as he sipped the drink like he didn't have a care in the world. "Excuse me."

"You're excused," he told her, taking another sip of his drink before setting his eyes on the astounded look on her face. "How about you tell me the real reason I haven't heard from you?"

"I'm always around if you ever needed me."

"I call bullshit," Legacy scoffed. "I used to re-up directly from you, and now you got some Italian moth-erfucka I don't know dropping off my supply. What's up with that? And then you changed your number and didn't give it out. What's up with that? Out of respect for you, I've respected your space. In the beginning, you and I were so close that Lace thought something was going on between us. Now she's asking every day when you and me are going to catch up, and I never have an answer. So what the fuck is up with that? After all I've done for you and The Last Kings, you owe me, if nobody else, an explanation. I thought we were family."

"There's nothing to explain," Sadie said, trying to keep all emotion from showing on her face. "I've been developing VEM. I got busy. I'm sorry."

"I call bullshit again. If it were that simple, you wouldn't have changed your number. You would have shot me a simple text and said, 'Hey, bro, I'm going off the radar for a few. I'll hit you when I resurface.' That's what you've done in the past."

"This time was different."

"The only thing different is that you're running from something," his deep voice said in a matter-of-fact tone. "It's obvious. The only question is, what exactly have you been trying to get away from?"

She had to look away from his piercing gaze. It was like he was analyzing her every movement, and she didn't like it. If he looked deep enough, he would find something that he wasn't supposed to.

"You of all people should know I don't run from anything," she said, turning away from him. She went to grab her glass from the sink. Suddenly she needed another drink.

"I *thought* you didn't run away from anything. There's a difference. In the wake of a drug like what you've created, I'd think that you would want everyone who has had a part in the success of this operation present and by your side. Unless the one who matters the most is missing," Legacy stated, and Sadie's face dropped.

She wished she had just kept her poker face, because when she and Legacy connected eyes again, it was like a light bulb had turned on above his head. She snatched the bottle from him and filled the small glass to the top.

"That's it, isn't it?" he asked and then let out a heavy breath. "This has nothing to do with you being busy. This has everything to do with that nigga Tyler. You still aren't over him, huh? How long has it been, six months?"

Sadie didn't say anything at first. Instead, she took a gulp of the alcohol and let it burn her throat until it hit her chest. She needed that uncomfortable slight pain to focus on at the moment. If she didn't have it, she feared that tears would well up in her eyes. Tyler's face popped up in her head, and suddenly she was angry.

"Do you know he made a Facebook page?" Sadie said out of nowhere. "When we were together, he never wanted to do the social media thing. He said that with everything we had at stake, it wouldn't be smart to be all over the internet, even though I told him it was weirder that we *weren't* on the internet. I mean, who isn't active online? But now, get this, he's on every social app with *her*. They've traveled all over the world, to almost as many places as he's taken me, and in six months, half a year, he proposed to her. We never even talked about marriage. And even though I know I'm the one who asked him for a break, that didn't mean go fall in love with somebody else. Now in any free time I have, I'm torturing myself watching him give her the life we had and the life we never will."

"Sadie—"

"I have to keep myself busy," she continued, interrupting him. "Because if I don't, I constantly ask myself, did he ever really love me if he moved on so fast? Were all these years nothing? Did they mean *nothing?* And until I stop asking myself those questions, it's just hard for me to be around anyone who reminds me of the time I spent with him. Including you. So there's your answer, Legacy, and I hope you're happy with it. Cheers."

She raised her glass in the air before downing the remainder of the liquid. She made a sour face as she swallowed, but the numbing sensation that came after made it worth it. Across the island, Legacy didn't say anything, but when she went to pour herself another glass, he took the bottle away from her.

"What, now I can't drink either?"

"Not if you're trying to numb emotions that you need to feel," Legacy said.

"Why do I need to feel emotions that hurt me?"

"Because they're a part of the motions you need to go through to get to where you need to be."

"Well, I don't want any part of them."

"Why do you think you constantly watch what he's doing with his new woman? Why do you think you care? It's because you haven't processed that it's over between the two of you. I think it is, anyway, since you haven't made a move to get him back. I'm assuming that you haven't talked to him?"

Sadie shook her head.

"Why not?"

"Because he seems happy."

"Looks can be deceiving," Legacy said casually, but the tone of his voice suggested he was hinting at something.

"You've seen him," Sadie said, studying his face. "Haven't you?"

"Maybe," Legacy told her, and when she cut her eyes at him, he nodded.

"Was she there?"

"Yes."

"What . . . what was she like?"

"Do you really want to know?" Legacy asked, looking her in the eyes. It was her turn to nod. "Jada is beautiful, kind, sweet, and she makes him laugh."

Sadie had never had a knife in her chest before, but it had to be like what Legacy's words made her feel like. Sadie knew the woman was pretty, but hearing her name out loud broke her. Tears appeared at the corners of her eyes, but Legacy wiped them away before they could completely fall down her cheeks.

"Even seeing all that, she still isn't you," he told her, placing his hand under her chin.

"What does that mean?"

"Go see for yourself . . . before it's too late." Legacy stood up and placed a kiss on her forehead. "Now I love you, sis, but if you ever go ghost like this again, I'll kill you. I'm about to go see about catching a flight home to my wife. And do me a favor? Take it easy on Ray. Truth be told, he wanted me to come check on you when he found out I would be in Detroit."

He threw the half-empty bottle of liquor away on his way out of the kitchen. When he got to the entranceway, Sadie called his name.

"What's up, sis?" He stopped to look at her over his shoulder.

"Give Lace my love," she said, and he flashed his straight, white teeth.

"Always."

And with that, he was gone.

Chapter 5

Later that night, in the darkness of her room, Ahli was entrapped in her own head. She lay on her side, facing the wall as a sea of thoughts rushed through her mind like a tidal wave. Ahli battled the confusion coursing through her body, mainly because Sadie had made a point to let her know that VEM was ready to be sold on the market. What she had failed to mention was that she meant in the U.S. Sadie hadn't said anything about VEM being sold already overseas, but then again, Sadie was the boss. She didn't *have* to tell anyone anything, and she had made that clear.

Ahli let out a sigh and opened the night table on the side of her bed. From it, she pulled out an old photo of her and her mom. Ahli had to have been about 2 years old in the picture, sitting on Rhebecca's lap, smiling big with a lollipop in one of her hands. They were on the steps of a house that Ahli didn't remember, but she knew her father had taken the photo because she saw his reflection in one of the windows. Rhebecca had been stunningly beautiful, and that was one of the things she'd passed down to her daughters. Ahli lay quietly, looking into her mother's eyes and wishing that, just for a second, she could have her back.

Ahli couldn't help but wonder how she would have turned out if she'd had a normal family life. She imagined herself as a music teacher, standing in front of a classroom of small children. But that daydream was cut short when she remembered that, even before she and Rhonnie were born, her parents had never lived normal lives. She and Rhonnie were never destined to be regular.

Her thoughts were interrupted by a soft tapping on her door. She wasn't sure if her ears were playing tricks on her, so she lay still and held her breath. After a few moments, the same tapping sounded again, and that time she got up from the bed. When she cracked open the door to see what Rhonnie wanted, she saw that it wasn't Rhonnie, but Brayland.

"I was on my way to the crib, but you were on my mind heavy," he told her with a sincere look in his eyes. When she didn't open the door wide enough for him to enter, he held a bottle of wine and two glasses up in the air. "I grabbed this from the cellar. I can't pronounce the name on it for shit, but it looks expensive."

Ahli bit the inside of her cheek as he shrugged his shoulders goofily. Fighting back the smiles he put on her face always proved to be the hardest task, and once again, she failed. Even in her moments of gloom, Brayland knew how to brighten her spirits. She couldn't lie, some company would be nice, and at one point in time, they *did* share Ahli's suite. When she opened the door all the way, the first thing Brayland did was whisk her into a deep kiss. The moment their lips touched, she felt herself melt into him.

"I thought I needed that more than you did, but maybe I was wrong," he said when their kiss broke.

"I thought today would be a relaxing day. Clearly, I was wrong," she sighed, closing the door behind him.

Once inside, Brayland took a seat on one of the sofa chairs in the corner of the large room. He opened the bottle of wine and filled the two glasses before placing it on the small table in front of him. After handing her a glass, his eyes went to something in her hand, and when she looked down, she saw that she was still holding the photo of her mother and her. He'd seen it many times, because she often pulled it out when she had a lot on her mind.

"You good?" he asked, concerned.

"I don't know," Ahli said and put the photo back where she'd gotten it from. "It's just a lot to process, I guess."

"VEM?"

"Yeah," she stated. "Shit's crazy."

"To be all the way real with you, after that first year of working for Sadie, I forgot all about it. Don't tell her I said this, but I don't think I ever thought it would work. I mean, when you first told me about it all those years ago, it sounded like a myth," Brayland said and made his voice go sarcastically deeper. "*Vita E Morte*. Life and death."

"It *was* a myth," Ahli said. "It was still a myth when I handed Sadie the formula, but apparently not."

"I just can't believe you didn't tell me about it. I didn't know we kept secrets from each other."

"Well, I would have told you if I had known about it myself."

"Wait, you mean Sadie ain't tell you?"

"Not until today," Ahli said.

"Damn." Brayland looked shocked. "The way y'all act sometimes, I would think you were the best of friends."

"I wouldn't go so far as to say that, but I can say that it shocked me that she just told me today. Especially since it's already being sold in Azua. Especially since . . ." Ahli let her voice trail off, and she sat in the chair opposite him and took a big sip of her wine.

"Especially since what?"

"I just can't help but think of my mom, you know?"

"What about her?"

"That she would be disappointed in me for giving the formula to anybody."

"You don't trust Sadie?"

"With my life."

"Then what's the problem?"

"What if . . . what if VEM was supposed to be hidden forever? I mean, my mom and my dad hid it for a reason. It was only by chance that I found it in the first place."

"Then they should have destroyed it," Brayland said like it wasn't rocket science, and Ahli's eyes shot daggers his way. "I'm just saying, baby. If that was the *only* documented recipe for a drug that shouldn't be on this earth, why was it still here? If it was so dangerous, why didn't they get rid of it when they had the chance to? Or even after that?"

"I don't know. But when my dad was struggling with us, before we got into the business we're into, why didn't he ever just go get it? If he had the solution to all of his money problems literally at his fingertips, why didn't *he* ever just fashion the drug? He would have turned my sister and me into walking weapons, and he chose not to rather than put a new drug on the market. That says a lot."

"You just said it yourself. He was struggling. You heard Sadie tonight. She had to hire the best scientists from around the world to make VEM."

Ahli sighed before speaking again. "When I first met Sadie, she was the one who told me what *Vita E Morte* was. She told me about the myth. She said the possessor of VEM could do two things: cause life or death."

"Because of the riches," Brayland stated.

"What?" Ahli asked, confused.

"I mean, think about it. This drug doesn't just have potential. It has the power to bring whoever owns it more money than any other drug ever could. You can bring new life if you got the paper for it. But then again, some people view money as the root of all evil because it's the cause of a lot of bad shit. Maybe that's what the myth means."

"Maybe," Ahli said, chewing on the inside of her cheek.

"Don't stress about it too much, my baby," he told her.

"My baby?" Ahli asked, amused because he had never called her that before.

"I've been here too long. These Detroit niggas got me talking like them," he said and grinned sheepishly.

He finished his glass of wine, placing it on the table next to the bottle, and focused his attention on Ahli. The gaze from his brown eyes was so piercing and intense that she almost wanted to look away, but she held it. She studied his face and thought about what he looked like when she had first met him. Gone was the lost boy with the high-top fade and blond tips. She was staring into the eyes of a man, her man. He'd said goodbye to the fade and welcomed a head full of natural curls that she loved to play in. His thick sideburns connected to the freshly trimmed mustache and short beard that were around his full lips. Rhonnie drove him crazy when she joked and called him an Odell Beckham Jr. wannabe, but to Ahli, he looked much better. He'd bulked up his build tremendously, and one of her favorite things to do was fall asleep in his arms. In fact, she loved it so much that him moving out was one of the hardest things to get used to. However, they both agreed that it would be a good idea for them to live like they were dating instead of living like they were married. Keeping their relationship fresh was always top priority. It went without saying that they still often spent their nights together, but they also gave each other their space.

"What you thinking about?" Ahli asked, breaking their eye contact finally to sip the last bit of her wine.

"You bouncing on this fat dick," Brayland said bluntly, causing Ahli to nearly spit her wine out.

"What!" she exclaimed.

"You asked, and I told you." His lips spread into a slow, mischievous smile. "It's your fault for looking so good in that suit."

"I wear suits daily. It can't be too sexy," she teased.

"Baby, you be wearing the hell out of them suits. Ass be poking like a bow!" He gestured his hands in a circular motion, and she laughed. "But, nah, for real, you gon' do that for me?"

"Do what?" Ahli feigned confusion.

"Aw, so that's how you gon' do me? I see how it is." Brayland pretended to be mad.

"I'm just playing, baby," Ahli said, letting the blazer of her suit fall back on the couch. "But if you want this pussy, I'm not riding shit. I put in all that work last night."

"I'll give you that," Brayland agreed.

Ahli squealed when he stood and scooped her up in his arms. She giggled when he laid her down on the bed, and she moaned when his lips and tongue found her neck. Her head nestled into her pillow, and she felt her entire body begin to tingle.

"A little salty, but that's all right." He grinned when he pulled away.

"I'll keep all this to myself then, since you're complaining," she said and placed her hands on his chest as if to push him off her.

"Girl, you know I like my meals seasoned," he said, removing her hands from his chest and placing them on his neck. "Go 'head and give me all this high blood pressure."

He placed his full, wet lips on hers, and they shared another kiss. They fondled each other hungrily as clothes began getting stripped off. Neither came up for air until they were both completely naked and Ahli felt his throbbing manhood between her legs. They had made love the night before, and right then, all Ahli wanted was a good fucking in every position they could until he exploded.

Her love tunnel was already drenched but became even more soaked when his mouth wrapped around her brown nipples. Her body arched as his tongue sucked and flicked over each of her areolas. Whichever nipple he wasn't sucking, he used his fingers to pinch it, sending pleasure vibrations down her spine. Her legs opened wider, giving him more access to her slippery cat. Her clit was thumping so hard, she was sure he could feel it on his torso.

"Boy, if you don't fuck me," she moaned.

"Like this?" he asked and slid two of his fingers deep inside of her.

Ahli's vaginal walls instantly clenched around them, and she inhaled a soft breath. Even though she would have preferred his chocolate dick, his long fingers digging in and out of her was pure bliss. Her love cries filled the air as he finger fucked her while still sucking her breasts. She didn't realize it, but her fingernails were digging into his shoulder blades, but he didn't make her stop. Just like her, he was focused on her climax, and he was willing to endure the small pain to get her there. It didn't take long for her clit to explode and thick juices to flow out of her tunnel and cover his hand.

"Fuck," he moaned when he withdrew his fingers. Not caring to wipe the cum off, he reached his hands around to grip her butt, and he lay on top of her. He placed his mouth by her ear and whispered, "Can I put it in?"

"Please," she begged.

She didn't have to say it twice, because within seconds, her pussy was filled with a thickness that his fingers could never compare to. He was the only man her body had ever known in that way, so she was molded to him. She made a hissing sound with her tongue as Brayland's dick fought against her walls to go as deep as it could.

"Ohhhh," she moaned and buried her head into his neck. "Braylannnd!"

"Shut up," he commanded. "I haven't even done nothing yet."

She loved when he talked to her like that, but only while they were having sex. There was something about being dominated in the bedroom that made her shiver. She couldn't get enough of it. Although she didn't mind taking control, she liked it better when he used her body to pleasure himself. It turned her on to see just how nasty he could be.

He started off stroking slowly, making their sex sound like a pot of macaroni being stirred. His hands kept squeezing her butt each time he thrust into her, and she heard his soft moans in her ear. Their bodies spoke the same language fluently, and she kissed his neck between her moans to encourage him. His strokes started to come faster and grow more powerful each time he plummeted into her.

"Braylannnd, right there," she cried, squeezing her walls. "It feels so good. Baby."

"Keep doing that," he instructed, and she did. "Damn, Ahli. I love this pussy. I love *you*."

"I love you too!" she cried.

"Shut up," he growled and placed his hand over her mouth as he looked animalistically into her eyes. "Take this dick and just shut the fuck up."

Her clit began to jump again as he beat her pussy into oblivion, and she couldn't do anything but take it. It wasn't just the fact that he was giving it to her so good, but the thought of the man she loved more than anything in the world being inside of her that brought her to an orgasm that time. She quivered from her head to the tips of her toes, and tears fell from her eyes because he never stopped pumping, and his hand was still over her mouth.

"I'm sorry I gotta do you like this, baby," he breathed into her ear, "but I know this is what you need. You work so hard, sometimes you just need a good fucking, huh? You wanted me to fuck this pussy just like this, didn't you?"

"Mm-hmm," she moaned.

She had wanted him to flip her into every position that he could think of, but as he dug into her missionary, she might have killed him if he stopped. Her back arched as yet another orgasm snuck up on her and beads of sweat dropped from her forehead. He finally removed his hand from her mouth, but he should have kept it there. The moment her lips were free, Ahli screamed words that weren't yet in the dictionary. In fact, they weren't even words. They were sounds that were meshed together. On top of her, she felt Brayland begin to quiver, and she knew what was about to happen. She clenched her walls around his shaft, and that time she didn't release until he quickly pulled out of her.

"Ahhh!" he shouted as he sat up quickly.

His hand stroked his dick feverishly, and he squirted his cum all over her bare breasts and stomach. When the last of the liquid was out, he stumbled to the bathroom to get a wet rag, and he wiped her off before collapsing beside her. Neither had the energy to do anything but climb under the covers and turn the light off with the remote switch on the nightstand. Ahli wanted to tell him how much she loved him, but he knew that. She wanted to tell him how much he meant to her, but he knew that too. So instead, she snuggled up to his chest and fell asleep to the rhythm of his breathing.

Chapter 6

Rhonnie had gotten up bright and early to take care of what Sadie had asked of her and Ahli. If she really wanted them to deliver product that day, that meant they had ten stops. Fully dressed, Rhonnie left her suite and stretched as she walked down to Ahli's quarters. Rhonnie always had felt that the mansion was based on an old English castle, from the wooden floors and the large portraits framed in gold along the walls all the way to the gold light fixtures that hung from the ceiling.

The wide windows lit the hallway brightly that morning, letting her know that it was going to be a warm spring day. Normally when it came down to business, Ahli was all over it. So Rhonnie was shocked that it was she waking Ahli up and not the other way around. As she passed the winding staircase between their quarters, the tall door to Ahli's suite opened, and Brayland stepped out. From the looks of it, he was still in last night's clothes, which meant he had stayed the night.

"I should have known." Rhonnie rolled her eyes. "What did you do, put her in a dick coma?"

"Has anybody ever told you how annoying you are?" Brayland groaned as he walked toward the staircase.

"I strive to hear those words from you every day." She smirked. "I think it's stupid that you left in the first place. I don't see why you don't just move back in."

"If me and Ahli ever get married, we'll cohabitate again. It's important for two people who spend so much time together to have their personal space, and our personal space just happens to be us living separately."

"That sounds like some bullshit my sister fed you," she said as he passed her, and by his glare, she might have been right.

"Nah, but it's not for you to understand. Maybe when you find a man who can tolerate you for more than a month, or who you don't have to kill, you'll understand."

"Ahli told you about Tim?" Rhonnie's mouth dropped open. She fought the urge to chase after him and punch him when he started laughing hysterically down the stairs.

Tim was a guy she had dated back in April. He had worked under Cam as one of his runners and had spent a lot of time and money trying to get Rhonnie's attention. She hadn't wanted to give him a chance, but when she did, she actually had a good time. He took her to an arcade for their first date, and it had been the first time in a long time that she had innocent fun. One day together turned into two weeks, and two weeks turned into four. She was playing with the thought of getting serious with him because, for one, he was already in the life, so that meant he understood her, and for two, even though she couldn't stand Brayland sometimes, she adored how he loved her sister. Low-key, Rhonnie wanted that kind of bond with somebody, and she thought Tim could be that somebody.

She was wrong.

In fact, she was so wrong, she almost cost Sadie a lot of headache. If Rhonnie hadn't gone through his phone one night while he was in the shower, and hadn't seen that he and someone were sending each other messages back and forth about Cam's plan to take down Sadie at the next payment drop, Sadie would have never switched locations at the last minute. When he took her home that night, Rhonnie was furious that he had just been using her that entire time. The first time in a long time that she'd let her guard down, he snaked her. She was so blind with rage that while they were driving to their date that evening, she grabbed the wheel. She swerved his Audi over a median into oncoming traffic and jumped out of the car. She suffered a sprained wrist and a few gashes on her arm, but he died. She had no regrets about it. The only thing she regretted at that moment was telling a sister who'd blabbed her personal business.

She didn't knock when she got to Ahli's suite. She just pushed the door wide open. Ahli was standing over her bed, putting her new Glocks in the holsters on her waist when Rhonnie intruded. Seeing her, Ahli started to smile, but upon recognizing the look on her face, she stopped.

"What happened? Is everything okay?" she asked, trying to make sense of Rhonnie's glare.

"*Why* does Brayland know about Tim?"

"Where is that coming from, NaNa?" Ahli made a face. "You two are always at each other's throats. It's really annoying."

"That's beside the point. Why are you discussing my personal business with him?"

"Because it was about a nigga who went against the family. He asked how we figured out Cam was moving foul, and I told him. I didn't think it would be that big of a deal."

"It *is* a big deal when a huge part of the story is about a motherfucka playing me!" Rhonnie exclaimed, angry that her sister didn't get it. "I'm in charge of protecting one of the biggest names in the game. Do you think I want people knowing that some dick had me gone? You could have said the same thing Sadie said about her having inside men. But no, you want to run your mouth."

"He is my man, and we don't keep secrets from each other." Ahli shrugged, unapologetic.

That was strange. Normally Ahli was the resolver of conflict, and she hated when Rhonnie was upset with her. But it seemed as if she couldn't care less at the moment. Rhonnie felt the small surge of anger inside of her subside and become replaced with worry. She studied the blank look on her sister's face to try to figure out what was wrong. When Ahli figured out what Rhonnie was doing, she turned away so she couldn't look as deeply.

"All right, spill it, LaLa," Rhonnie told her, not up for playing games. "What's wrong with you? Did Bray do something?"

"No."

"Then why are you acting all . . . weird?"

"I'm not."

"Yes, you are." Rhonnie wasn't letting her off that easily. "First at the hotel, then at the meeting. You've been acting like this ever since Sadie told us *Vita E Morte* was ready. Is that it? Are you mad that she actually made it? Because you're the one who—"

"Told her where it was," Ahli interrupted her and sighed deeply. "I know. It's all still just processing, that's all."

"What about it has to process?"

"I mean, it doesn't feel strange to you?" Ahli asked, plopping down on the bed. "Our parents—"

"Hid it for a reason? I know. But maybe they just didn't want Madame to have it. I mean, the bitch *was* crazy."

"You don't think there is a possibility that it's something else?"

"You watched the video just like I did. Those people were loving it. We might be on to something, and I don't know about you, but I like living like this." Rhonnie waved her hands around Ahli's room.

"We were living like this before."

"Well, more money is never a bad thing. I thought you would understand that."

"I do, I just—"

Knock, knock. "Am I interrupting a sister moment?"

The girls looked up and saw Sadie standing at Ahli's doors. Her hair lay over her shoulders, and she was wearing a robe and nightgown like she had no plans of leaving the mansion anytime soon. Her sharp brown eyes flicked back and forth between them curiously, as if she were trying to figure out what they had been discussing.

"No, you aren't. We were just getting ready to leave," Ahli spoke before Rhonnie could. "Rhonnie was just telling me that maybe we should hit our distributors today by splitting up."

She shot Rhonnie a look as if to tell her to shut up, which was unlike her. Although they were closer to each other, they had always been open with Sadie, especially when it came to them feeling indifferent about anything. But Rhonnie didn't reference what they were talking about. Instead, she nodded as if agreeing with Ahli.

"Yeah," she said. "That way we'll get done faster and can be back just in case you need us."

Sadie eyed them both for a few more moments before a smile formed on her face. She gave them an approving head gesture. "Smart," she said. "I can always count on the two of you to think innovatively. I'll have someone split up the load for you so you can take two vans and not one."

"Yeah." Rhonnie forced a little laugh. "Leave it to us to think inno . . . what you just said."

Ahli rolled her eyes and stood up. "I'll take Rashad and all the niggas near that side. You take Jaq and the people near his side," she told Rhonnie and headed for the door.

"I'll send you both a video to show them exactly what they'll be selling."

"All right," Ahli said. Before she left, she looked at Sadie and said, "Call me if you need anything else."

When she was gone, Rhonnie made to leave as well, but when she tried to pass, Sadie put a hand out to stop her. "Rhonnie."

"Yeah?"

"Is there anything you want to tell me?" Sadie's stare was even more piercing up close and in person, and Rhonnie tried to keep her face as emotionless as possible.

"About what?" She feigned innocence.

"About Ahli. Is everything all right with her? If she's trying to hide her frustrations, she's doing a terrible job. It's no confidential matter that she isn't as excited about VEM as everyone else."

"She will be all right. I think she might be on her period or something," Rhonnie said and shrugged her shoulders, but Sadie didn't look like she bought that for one second.

"I need you to keep an eye on her for me," Sadie told her. "Can you do that for me?"

Spy on her own sister? It wasn't like she hadn't done it before, but that was more for her own personal gain. And she hadn't done it since they were younger when she used to blackmail Ahli to not tell on her to their father.

Something about Sadie asking seemed wrong, unethical even. Especially since Sadie often said they were two of her most trusted. Rhonnie's eyebrow twitched to raise, but she made sure it stayed in place. Maybe Ahli was right. About what? Rhonnie didn't know, but the hairs on the back of her neck were standing up. Something wasn't right.

"Of course," she said and smiled at her boss before leaving.

She felt Sadie's eyes on the back of her head the whole way to the winding staircase. When she was finally out of sight, she let out a breath that she'd been holding. Trying to put the exchange to the back of her mind, she made her way to the garage. Once she was there, she saw that Sadie must have already made the call, because two men were unloading five duffle bags from one Mercedes transit van to the next. The side of the van bore the name SHINE LUXURY BATHROOM APPLIANCE, which was a real company Sadie owned. Ahli was leaned against the one they were unloading from, and she texted on her phone. When she saw Rhonnie approaching, she stood up straight.

"Hey, we can make the runs together if you want," she said. "I only said we were going to do them separately because it was the first thing that came to my head."

"No, it's actually a smart idea," Rhonnie told her. "She hasn't said she needs us for anything else, so the sooner I can get back home, the better."

"Cool. We should be done by one if we leave now. Let's meet somewhere for lunch when we're done, cool?"

"Cool with me," Rhonnie said, avoiding eye contact. She hoped that her sister didn't notice. She hadn't known how to tell Sadie the truth about Ahli's feelings, nor did she know how to tell Ahli that their boss wanted her to be watched. She would rather tiptoe around both facts for as long as she could. Luckily, Ahli didn't seem to notice Rhonnie's behavior. She was too busy on her phone.

Once the vans were both loaded and ready to go, the girls went their separate ways. It wasn't the first time they had worked alone, but it *was* their first time making product drops alone. Rhonnie was confident that everything would be everything. Plus, she was eager to see what everyone was saying about Cam since he had been laid to rest. She figured she would go out and then work her way back into Detroit.

Her first three stops went according to schedule. She got the money, and they got the work. Her second-last stop was in Troy, Michigan to a young hustler named Cleo. He was in his early twenties, like her, and was always eager to put in work for Sadie. He was eager to move up in the ranks and was loyal. He also had a thing for Rhonnie, and he let it be known, but *she* let it be known that she wasn't interested. She didn't like him in that way, and not just because Tim had been somewhat of a colleague to him.

Cleo may have been a lot of women's cup of tea, but he wasn't hers. For one, she didn't find him attractive. He was chocolate, how she liked her men, but his eyes were a little too close together, and one of them drooped a little bit. They were the same height, and his beard struggled to connect with his sideburns. Also, he was missing a tooth, and whenever he smiled, that was all she seemed to see. With all the money he was getting, she didn't understand why he wouldn't go and take care of that.

When she arrived at his two-story brick house, she grabbed a duffle bag from the back before getting out of the van. Cleo lived in a nice neighborhood where the houses were a good distance apart. She took notice of the surveillance cameras recording the front perimeter of the home, and she also saw his dog, Paco, leap off the porch as she approached. Paco was a Blue Nose Pitbull that liked to act tough whenever she had to stop by. He began to bark loudly and bared his teeth when his chain prevented him from going as far as he would have liked. He might have scared others, but not Rhonnie.

"Shut up," she said, glaring at him as she passed, and instantly Paco lay down in the grass and began to whimper. "That's what I thought."

When she got to the door, she rang the doorbell once and waited for someone to answer. She could smell the aroma of chicken being fried, and she heard a lot of chatter going on. After a few moments, the door swung open, and Cleo greeted her with a smile.

"Don't be smiling at me. Got me out here waiting like you ain't know I was coming." Rhonnie rolled her eyes and moved him out of the way when she entered the house.

Cleo seemed to be having a little lunch party, because his home was full of men and women. Rhonnie glanced in the living room area and saw people watching something on the television and passing a blunt around. A woman Rhonnie didn't recognize came from the back of the house to where they were. She was light-skinned with a blond lace-front wig and was wearing a skin-tight dress. Rhonnie could tell by the stank look on her face that she was a little ghetto thing. There was no class in the way she walked. She looked Rhonnie up and down with a distasteful expression and put a hand on her hip.

"Who is this, Cleo?" she asked in a squeaky voice. "I thought I told you to tell your bitches not to stop by today.

It's my birthday. I'm in there cooking all this food, and this is what you're out here doing?"

"Peaches, take your thot ass back in the kitchen, a'ight? I'm handlin' business," Cleo told her, looking annoyed.

"Business my ass," Peaches said. She turned to head back to where she'd come from, but not before throwing in one last bit. "Cheap suit–wearing bitch. You always fucking with some bitches who ain't got shit on me."

Rhonnie had to hold in a laugh at the comparison. Rhonnie easily was wearing $60,000, if you included the Audemars Piguet on her wrist, but she didn't expect a hood rat to understand that.

"My bad, Rhonnie," Cleo said, rubbing a hand over his brush cut. "That bitch is so ghetto."

"I can see, but you love you a ratchet bitch, don't you?" Rhonnie gave him a knowing look.

"I mean, you could change all that, though," Cleo told her with a sly smirk.

"Boy, you better stop before she comes and cuts your dick off with some kitchen shears," Rhonnie said.

"Man, you tripping! Come upstairs to my office so we can handle this business," he laughed and waved her toward the stairs.

She didn't want to be there too long because the last thing she wanted was to leave his house smelling like chicken. After she followed him to his office, she placed the duffle bag on one of the couches and unzipped it. She tossed one of the cocaine kilos to him and then took out the small Baggie of pills.

"What's that?" he asked after inspecting the kilo. "E?"

"Nah, something better than that," she said and shook the Baggie in the air. "This right here is the future."

"Well, I only thought I was buying my usual bricks."

"No worries. These are compliments of Sadie," Rhonnie said and tossed the pills to him. "They're called VEM, and she wants them on the streets ASAP. A hundred a pop, but you can work this first batch however you want since it's new."

"Word? Must be some good shit."

"Indeed," she said and went into the whole spiel of what exactly the drug was.

Just like she'd done at her other stops, Rhonnie pulled out her phone to show him the video Sadie had sent to her. It was a clip from the one they'd watched at the meeting the night before. She watched the interest on Cleo's face grow, especially when she said the high lasted for days.

"If this does everything the bitch on that video says it does, I'll be back." He nodded approvingly. "I will definitely be back for more."

Rhonnie almost wanted to tell him to tell her if he heard about anything negative happening as well, but she didn't. Instead, she stood by for him to hand her a bag of money and a money counter. After letting the machine do its thing and confirming it was all there, Rhonnie left. When she was back in the van, the first thing she smelled was the fried food on her clothing, and she smacked her lips.

"Black folks always cooking chicken," she said and pulled off from the house.

As she drove to the last drop spot, her mind went back to the meeting from the night before. She didn't find it strange at the time that she was giving VEM away for free, because the men at the table were bosses on the level of Sadie. But the fact that she was giving it to her underbosses for free was mindboggling. Even when she got new product in, Sadie never fronted anyone because she was always confident in her product. If you wanted to do any kind of business with Sadie, money was the thing that talked before she ever heard the words coming from your mouth.

As Rhonnie pondered the meeting, her thoughts fell on the youngest of the men at the table. Cyril, she remembered, was his name. He was handsome. No, the boy was fine as hell, with his smooth chocolate skin and his tapered fade. He had looked to be around her age, but maybe a little younger. However, the aura around him spoke loudly. For him to have even been at the table meant that Sadie thought highly of him. Curiosity got the best of her, and at the next red light, she found herself scrolling online, trying to find a profile that matched him.

Although the world thought she was dead, that didn't mean she didn't have a fake profile when she wanted to see what the people around her were doing. She thought it would be easy, because Cyril didn't seem like a common name, but unfortunately, there were a lot of them. It took her scrolling during three more red lights to finally find him, and it didn't seem like he was online often.

His profile picture was of him smiling with an older guy who resembled him. By doing some more scrolling, she found out that the man in the photo was his late brother, Cane. Rhonnie's heart instantly went out to him, because she didn't know what she would do if she ever lost Ahli. She almost did, but Rhonnie had risked her own life to save her older sister.

She could tell that he was a private person, probably because of the life he lived, but he did share some things with the world, like his love for basketball and how much he missed his big brother. But for the most part, he was a ghost. She liked ghosts.

She reached her last destination and turned into the condo parking lot. When she parked, she glanced back down at the phone in her hand and saw that her thumb had accidently hit the **Send Message** button on his profile. She made to click out of it and go inside, but she paused.

"What are you doing?" she asked herself aloud. "Don't do it, Rhonnie."

But she was terrible at taking her own advice. Her interest in him had spiked, and if they were going to be working together anyway, what was the harm in getting to know him, right? Before she knew it, she had typed out a message.

Hey, this is Rhonnie from last night. Hit this number and delete this message.

She attached her number and sent it quick so she didn't lose her nerve. Why was she nervous? It felt like she was in middle school, writing her crush on Myspace for the first time. She smiled because of the butterflies in her stomach. She couldn't remember the last time she'd felt them.

Rhonnie snapped out of her little daze and reached behind her to grab the last duffle bag from the back, and she got out. The last drop was for Jaquies Romano, aka Jaq. He'd been working for Sadie for a little over a year. He never shorted on his payment, and he always got his work off quickly. He was another one who was trying to move up in the ranks, and now that Cam was out of the picture, there was a vacancy.

As she walked to the entrance of the condo, she glanced up to where Jaq's unit was. On his balcony, looking back down at her, was a big man who put her in mind of a gorilla. She shook the bag on her shoulder and pointed at the door.

"You just gon' stare at me or are you gon' let your boss know that I'm here?" she asked.

He gave a short laugh before nodding and going back inside. Soon after, Rhonnie heard the soft buzz that let her know she could pull the door open. She went up three flights of stairs, and when she got to Jaq's unit, he was already standing in the doorway. He was a yellow-skinned man with long hair that he kept braided. He was handsome. Some would even call him pretty because of his smooth baby face, wide, bright eyes, and pink lips. He casually rocked a Balenciaga T-shirt and jeans, and he had a joint hanging from his lips. He glanced over his gold Cartier frames behind and around her before giving her a shocked expression.

"No partner in crime today?" he asked, and she knew he was referring to Ahli.

"No, is that a problem?" Rhonnie asked.

"Nope," he said and moved back so she could enter.

As soon as she entered, she almost choked on all the smoke that entered her lungs. The entire front area of the condo was a cloud of smoke. Rhonnie counted five men on the couch, including the one who had been on the balcony, and one in the kitchen going through the fridge. They were partaking in a smoking session, and Rhonnie wanted to roll her eyes. Not only would she smell like chicken, but now her clothes would hold the aroma of a whole pound of marijuana.

"Where are we doing this at?" she asked to speed things up.

"In a rush?" Jaq asked, lighting the joint in his mouth. "You don't want to hit this right quick?"

"I don't smoke," she told him and turned her nose up. "I'm here on business, and I would like to get to it if you don't mind."

"A'ight, I feel you," he said and pointed to the tall, wooden dining room table. "You can set that shit right there. Let me go grab the paper."

He disappeared, and while he was gone, the eyes of a few of his men shot her way. Whenever she looked back, they looked away, and she didn't like that. She felt the hairs on the back of her neck stand up and wanted Jaq to hurry up so she could get out of there. Her stomach was growling, and she was sure Ahli was done with her rounds already. She reached in her pocket to grab her phone but realized that she'd left it in the car.

"All right, it should all be there, but you can run it through the counter to make sure," Jaq said, placing the bag of money and a counter on the table.

"Cool," was all she said and began the count.

When she confirmed that it was, in fact, all there, she placed all the money back in the bag he had given her. She then slid the duffle bag with the drugs across the table to him. She watched him open it and inspect the bricks before nodding his approval. His eyes fell to the Baggie of pills that sat on top of the ten kilos of cocaine, and his brow furrowed.

"What's this? I didn't know I was going to be pushing anything else." He picked the bag up and held it up in the air to get a closer look at it.

"That right there will give your customer a high that they've never had. A high that lasts longer than any they've ever experienced and doesn't come with the same side effects. They go for one hundred a pop, and that bag there is courtesy of Sadie."

"For real?" he asked, seeming more than interested when she told him how much the pills went for. "What's the name of these pills, Rhon?"

"It's Rhonnie," she corrected him. "And it's VEM, short for *Vita E Morte.* It stands for—"

"Life or death," he finished for her, suddenly looking mesmerized at the bag.

"You've heard of it?" It was her turn to wrinkle her forehead in surprise.

"My pops is Italian," Jaq explained. "When I was coming up in the game, he used to talk about the forbidden drug called Life or Death. He said the person who possessed it would run and ruin the world."

"Was that . . ." Rhonnie cleared her throat. "Was that all he said?"

Instead of answering her question, he stood there with a stunned expression on his face. No. The closer Rhonnie looked, she saw that it wasn't just shock. It was fear. She had to nudge him to snap him out of his daze.

"Did you hear me?" she asked him. "Was that all he said?"

"Just that it shouldn't exist. That it would be better to poison the world with crack and cocaine than to ever put *Vita E Morte* on the streets. I thought it was just a myth, but I never saw my pops seem afraid of anything, but this shit? He wasn't fucking with." Jaq shook his head and gave Rhonnie the bag back. "So I can't fuck with it either. I'll move these bricks all day and any other pill, but not that."

Rhonnie didn't know what to say when she took the Baggie back. But she could feel that the climate in the air had shifted. In fact, Jaq had taken a few steps back. It was apparent that he didn't want anything to do with the bag of pills in Rhonnie's hand. She figured that was her cue to leave. She nodded at him and grabbed the bag of money on the table before making her exit.

When she was back in the van and the money was safe and sound, Rhonnie checked the phone she'd left in the cupholder. She had two unread messages, and one was from Ahli. She was just telling Rhonnie to meet up at The Last Kings' main stash spot when she was finished. Rhonnie sent her a message back, telling her that she was on the way. The other message was from an unsaved number, and when she clicked it open, she saw that it was Cyril. After the exchange inside the condo, she had forgotten that she'd even reached out to him.

Hey, this is Cyril. Lock me in.

She didn't know how to reply because the butterflies she'd felt in her stomach before had flown away. Rhonnie locked the phone and let it fall in her lap. She'd thrown the bag of VEM in the passenger's seat but took that moment to pick them back up. Weighing the Baggie in her hand, she wondered how she would tell Sadie that Jaq refused to distribute the pills. His words played over and over in her head. It seemed like a dark cloud was looming over her, and the first thing that came to mind was Ahli. Had she been right to have her suspicions about the drug? Sadie had put Rhonnie in the position to pick a side, and she had made her decision. She was going to ride with her sister until the wheels fell off. Rhonnie decided that she wouldn't tell Sadie that Jaq had refused the drug. She was going to take the pills to Ahli.

Chapter 7

Ahli pulled the van she was driving into a car wash called Squeaky Cleaners for a quick wash. As soon as the Mercedes transit was seen pulling in, an older man with a caramel complexion came out of the white brick building. He was tall and resembled Method Man from his build all the way to the hair on his face. He approached the vehicle, and when Ahli got out, he welcomed her with a warm smile and embrace.

"How you doing, Lem?" she asked, giving him a pat on the back before being released from the hug.

"I can't complain. But what's good with you, my baby? No Rhonnie today?"

"She just hit me not too long ago," Ahli said, squinting her eyes up the road to see if any of the cars driving by were her sister. When none of them was a transit van, she shrugged and handed him the keys to hers. "She should be here shortly."

"No problem. What can I do for you today?"

"I need a full detail," she said, giving him a knowing look. "And when Rhonnie gets here, she'll need the same."

"No worries, I got you," Lem said, not missing a beat and made to get into the vehicle. "This might take a while, so you can take one of the courtesy vehicles in the back."

"I'm not trying to push no fucking red Volkswagen Jetta today, Lem," Ahli told him, and he chuckled.

"I guess it's a good thing I have that new 2020 Chevy Trailblazer back there. Black, just like you like them," Lem stated. "Just go up in there, and Petey Boy will get you taken care of."

"You need to get some luxury vehicles," Ahli grumbled before walking away, and she heard him chuckle again.

He pulled the van past the regular washing station to the back of the shop and into a detached garage where the detail center was. Once the van was inside, the garage door closed, and Ahli knew exactly what was taking place without even needing to see it. Squeaky Clean wasn't a business that Sadie laundered through. It was where she hid large amounts of money until it *could* be laundered. The detail center sat on top of a basement that wasn't in any of the blueprints of the property. It was undocumented, so it didn't exist.

At that moment, Ahli could guess that Lem was grabbing the bags of money and taking them to that basement. After that was done, he would clean the inside of the vehicle to make sure there was no residue from any drug paraphernalia. Then he would make one of his workers take it back to the regular wash station to wash the outside down. While they did that, he'd go back to the basement and conduct his own count of the money. Once he was done, he would contact Sadie and tell her the number. Sadie never told him the number she expected to hear, Ahli had found out through Lem. And she figured maybe that was so Lem couldn't warn whoever made the drop if the count was off.

Ahli went inside to grab a set of car keys from Petey Boy, who *knew* he was wrong for letting people still call him "boy." He was a grown man with gray hair, a gray beard, and a mouthful of dentures. Maybe the name helped him keep his youth. With that being said, he was one of the sweetest people Ahli had ever met, and he always gave her candy when she stopped in. The door chimed when she opened it, and she saw that he was sitting behind the front desk wearing his usual dirty work overalls and a hat on his head. He'd been reading a newspaper and drinking a beer, but he set the drink down when he saw Ahli standing at the desk.

"There she go!" he shouted with a smile. "Where the hell you been, girl?"

"I've been working, Petey Boy," Ahli said, returning his smile. "You sure you supposed to be drinking on the job?"

"Fuck these people! As long as they get their damned cars cleaned, they better not say shit to me. 'Cause I can't get fired, you hear me, niece?"

"Loud and clear." Ahli grinned because it was obvious he was a little tipsy.

"You want some candy?"

"You got some of them sour Warheads?" she said, humoring him.

"Do I?" Petey Boy gave her a look that said, "Are you crazy?"

From his pocket, he pulled a handful of wrapped candy and held his palm out to her. She pretended to ponder which she wanted before grabbing a red one and pocketing it. She never ate the candy, but he didn't know that.

"Lem said y'all got a 2020 Trailblazer back there for me."

"Yeah, we do, and that thing is a piece of shit!"

"Petey Boy!"

"All right, all right. It's not a piece of shit," he admitted and handed her the key fob. "But dammit, if that motherfucka Lem don't get somethin' of luxury quality back there for y'all, I'm gon' kick his ass myself."

Ahli had tears in her eyes from laughing so hard. Petey Boy was like that favorite black uncle at the family barbecue. He didn't have a filter to save his life, and he didn't care either.

"What's so funny?" a new voice asked after the doorbell sounded.

Ahli turned around while wiping her eyes and saw that Rhonnie had finally gotten there. She had to take a few deep breaths before she could talk again, but when she did, she pointed at Petey Boy. "I'm laughing at his crazy ass. You know how he gets."

"Rhonnie!" Petey Boy exclaimed and then made a face. "Girl, why you lookin' like somebody stole your purse and it had all your shit in it? What's wrong?"

Ahli had been so focused on trying to stop laughing that she hadn't even taken in her sister's expression. She didn't look mad or happy, just indifferent. Instantly, all the humor left Ahli's body as she thought something bad had happened on the run.

"Did everything go all right?" she asked.

"Yeah, I'm just hungry is all," Rhonnie said, but Ahli could tell she was lying by the shift in her eye contact.

"Okay," was all Ahli said right there. She waved a hand at Petey Boy. "It was good seeing you. We'll have someone come grab the vans when Lem is done."

"Okay. You two have a blessed day. I'm about to get on up to the hospital to see Tina's crazy ass."

They didn't pay his last words much mind. They just walked around the desk and left out the back of the car wash. Parked right in front of them and squeaky clean was the SUV they would be taking. Ahli didn't feel like driving anymore, but judging by Rhonnie's demeanor, she didn't either. Ahli just bit the bullet and got in the driver's seat. She waited until they'd pulled out of the parking lot and were on the road to glance quickly over at Rhonnie.

"What you got a taste for? I could eat some hot wings."

"Because you always have a taste for chicken," Rhonnie told her, staring out her window.

"And you usually do too," Ahli said. "What else do you want to eat then?"

"It doesn't matter. Hot wings are cool."

It was the dryness in her response that made Ahli abruptly pull to the side of the road and park.

"Okay, please tell me, what happened? Did one of them niggas try to short you?" Ahli asked and mentally prepared to go to war with whoever for whatever reason.

"You know these niggas aren't stupid, LaLa." Rhonnie gave her a look that said Ahli should have known better.

"All right, then tell me, what's wrong? This morning it was me with the attitude, and now it's you. What's your problem?"

"The same problem you have," Rhonnie admitted and then tossed something on Ahli's lap

When she looked down, Ahli recognized it as a bag of VEM. She picked it up, not understanding how Rhonnie still had it, since they were supposed to deliver them. But before she could open her mouth to ask, Rhonnie already was answering.

"Those were supposed to be Jaq's," she said. "But he didn't want them."

"He didn't want free drugs?" Ahli was even more confused.

"No, he didn't. He knew what they were." Rhonnie looked her sister in the eyes. "His father is Italian and told him about *Vita E Morte* a long time ago. He called it the forbidden drug."

"The forbidden drug?" Ahli asked, and Rhonnie nodded. "Why?"

"I don't know, but he looked scared, LaLa."

"Jaq?" Ahli was shocked mainly because she had seen what he could do when tested. "Jaq looked . . . scared?"

"Yep. He said he would rather poison the streets with crack and cocaine than push VEM. He didn't want anything to do with those pills."

"Did you tell Sadie?"

"No." Rhonnie gave her sister a guilty look.

"What did you do then?" Ahli asked.

"I didn't do anything!" Rhonnie exclaimed, looking offended and then guilty all over again. "Well, besides not tell you something. This morning, after you left, Sadie stopped me and asked me to do something."

"Okay, she's our boss. She always asks us to do something."

"But this something has to do with you. She knows something is off with you, sister, when it comes to VEM. And she asked me to keep an eye on you."

"What?" Ahli asked and felt her heart drop to her stomach. "She asked you to spy on me?"

Rhonnie nodded, and Ahli was speechless. The only people who had a reason to not trust her were her enemies, but Sadie? She had never given her a reason to

feel that way. Ahli felt surges of hurt and anger coursing through her body. Her hand tightened around the
drugs, and she tried to regain her composure. Beside her,
Rhonnie could tell that she was upset and placed a hand
on her shoulder as if to tell her things would be okay.

"Was that all she asked?" Ahli asked when she calmed
down, and Rhonnie nodded. "Why didn't you tell me that
this morning?"

"Because your ass is crazy!" Rhonnie told her. "And I
couldn't believe I got put in the middle of it."

"Were you going to do it?"

"What? Spy on you? I'm always in your business, you
know that. But report it to her? No. I love Sadie, but
you're my sister. You've been here since my first breath."

Ahli believed her, but that didn't make her any less
angry. She let all of the new knowledge process and
looked down at the bag of pills. *The forbidden drug?*
"Why did you bring these to me?"

"I don't know, because you're the smart one," Rhonnie
said with a shrug. "What do you want to do?"

Ahli pondered the question, even though the answer
was obvious.

"I want to talk to Jaq's father."

It took a few days' worth of digging to gather the information that would lead Ahli and Rhonnie to the
whereabouts of Jaq's father. They had to use their influence over a few moles The Last Kings had working
as government officials. The sisters knew they could
have just asked Jaq, but neither wanted to risk it getting
back to Sadie what they were doing. Especially since
they both asked for a leave of absence for three days af-

ter finding out that he resided in Cleveland, Ohio. They didn't know what they were going to find and wanted to give themselves time to process or prepare for anything thrown their way.

From the information they'd gathered, they knew Angelo Romano was in his early fifties. His wife had died three years prior, so he lived in their home all alone. Outside of Jaq, they also had a daughter named Jolanda, who was a few years older than him. Angelo was retired, so he spent most of his time reading on the balcony in his backyard or fishing in a lake near his home.

After making the two-hour drive, the girls went directly to the address they had listed for him. The sun had started to go down when their car pulled around the circular driveway and parked behind an Audi. Both Rhonnie and Ahli were dressed casually instead of wearing their usual suits.

"We don't want him to think the Men in Black are at his door," Rhonnie had said.

And whereas Ahli agreed with not wearing a suit, she thought her sister was an idiot for comparing them to the Men in Black. Anybody with eyes could tell that the suits she and Rhonnie wore were much better. They got out of Rhonnie's Rolls-Royce and made their way to the front door, which swung open before they had a chance to knock. Standing in the foyer of the home, looking at them over a pointed nose, was a pretty young woman wearing work scrubs. Her long black hair hung in loose curls down to the middle of her back, and her hazel eyes surveyed them curiously.

"Oh." Rhonnie's eyes showed that she hadn't expected that. "We didn't even get the chance to ring the doorbell."

"Well, it's not every day a Rolls-Royce pulls up to your father's house. Can I help you?"

"You must be Jolanda," Ahli said and tried to give her a warm smile.

"It's always a good thing when someone knows who you are, but you've never seen them a day in your life," Jolanda said sarcastically.

"We're friends of Jaq," Ahli said in hopes that would lighten the mood, but if anything, it made Jolanda look more concerned.

"What has that brother of mine gotten himself into this time?"

"Nothing bad," Ahli told her, taking note of the hint of annoyance in Jolanda's tone. "We were just wondering if your father, Angelo, was home. We had a few questions for him."

"Are you Feds?" Jolanda asked and looked from Rhonnie to Ahli.

"Girl, do you think a Fed would be able to afford all this drip?" Rhonnie spat out, clearly offended, and Ahli shot her a look.

"Excuse my sister. No, we aren't Feds," Ahli assured Jolanda. "Like I said, we're *friends* of Jaq."

"Mmm, figures." Jolanda pursed her lips and crossed her arms. "No wonder you can afford all that . . . what did you just call it? Oh, yeah, *drip*. You bought it with all that dirty money."

"The same dirty money he gave your father so he could buy this house," Rhonnie shot back.

"The same money my father gave right back," Jolanda said through clenched teeth, as if Rhonnie had just said the most insulting thing in the world. "You don't know my brother the way we do. My father didn't want blood money."

"Blood money or drug money?" Rhonnie asked.

"Both."

"Listen, we just came to talk to Angelo. Is he here?" Ahli asked, growing impatient.

After a few more moments of hard stares, Jolanda finally sighed and waved them inside of the house. It smelled like someone had been in the kitchen making lasagna, or maybe it was spaghetti. The inside of the house was gorgeous, with its stained wooden floors and high ceilings. There were family portraits hung on all the walls, and Ahli was curious as to what the U-shaped staircase led to.

"He's in his study. Down there and to your right. The door should be open." Jolanda pointed down the hallway of the large home. "I wish I could tell you that he grew kind in his old age, but he's still the meanest motherfucker I know. So whatever it is you want to talk to him about, be direct. He hates it if he feels like you're wasting his time."

She closed the front door and went back to doing whatever she'd been doing. They followed her instructions and were able to find Angelo's study easily. There, sitting at a computer desk, was an older gentleman puffing on a cigar. His back was to them, so Ahli rapped on the door with her knuckles before they entered to announce their presence.

"Friends of my son's, huh?" Angelo asked in a deep baritone voice. He didn't turn around in his seat. Instead, he just kept on puffing. "I may not be young like I used to be, but I have the hearing of a bat. To what do I owe this pleasure?"

"My name is Ahli, and this is my sister Rhonnie, and we work for—"

"The Last Kings, I figured," he interrupted. "Go on."

"We came to ask you some questions."

"Obviously. Did you come all this way to beat around the bush?"

Be direct, Ahli thought. "Okay, the truth is we came to ask you about *Vita E Morte*," she spat out and watched Angelo stop smoking mid-puff.

Slowly, he spun around in his chair to face them, and the expression on his face was hard to read. He looked exactly like Jaq, just older and with short hair. The lit cigar hung between his fingers, and he let the ash fall to the floor.

"We heard you know something about it, and we came to ask," Ahli continued when he didn't say anything.

"*Vita E Morte* is a myth. What you young folks call an old urban legend," he said and tried to chuckle, but it didn't come out.

"We know a little bit about the myth. But it isn't one anymore," Rhonnie said, pulling the Baggie of pills from her pocket and tossing it to him. "The Last Kings created it."

"W . . . what?" Angelo's hand was shaky as he looked down at the drug. "No, it can't be. I don't believe it."

"Well, believe it."

"Do you know what you've done?"

"No," Ahli told him. "That's what we're here to find out. Our boss has started distributing those pills already, but your son Jaq refused to sell them."

"I knew that boy had some kind of sense," Angelo said and then sighed. "And I guess you're here to figure out why he wouldn't touch them."

"Yes. He looked afraid when I showed him that same bag you're holding," Rhonnie explained.

"And he should have been. *You* should be scared too." Angelo stared closely at the pills. "The forbidden drug, but how?"

"Our mother had the formula for it, and I . . . well, I gave it to our boss," Ahli admitted. "And then our boss had it created in a lab."

"So then, this is your fault." Angelo glared at her. "Everything that is about to happen will be on your hands."

"What does that mean? What's about to happen?"

"Death," he said simply, sending chills up Ahli's spine.

"Can you tell us the myth *you* know, the same as you told your son?" Ahli asked.

Angelo's eyes became glossy, as if he were lost in a trance for a second. When he came back, he looked deeply in Ahli's eyes and began speaking as if he were reciting a story.

"A long time ago, in Italy, there was a woman by the name of Giovanna Bianchi. She was born to a very rich family but had fallen in love with a simple sheepherder. As long as the two of them stayed in Italy, they would never be able to be together. See, Giovanna's father wanted his daughter to marry into a wealthy family. In fact, she was already promised to another. So imagine the rage her father felt when he found out that his only daughter had been running around with the sheepherder. Her father asked Giovanna's mother to keep her busy while he and her brothers murdered the sheepherder while he napped. Poor Giovanna thought that her lover had run off without her, so she was forced to marry the man whom her father saw fit.

"When Giovanna found out about her father's treachery, she vowed to make him and everyone involved pay. So she went to visit the town's witch who helped her concoct a formula, but not a poison. You see, Giovanna thought that would be too easy. She wanted her family to feel exactly how she felt. She wanted them to suffer slowly. The drug that the witch helped her create targeted specific parts of the human brain and body. They called it *Vita E Morte,* life and death. Once swallowed or injected, the person affected would instantly become addicted. And upon taking more doses, they would feel their bodies go through stages.

"The first stage, the person would feel inexplicably blissful. That lasted for about forty-eight hours' time before it wore off, but by then, the user was already addicted and needing more and more until they reached the second stage: complete dependency to the point where the body would be in complete agony if it didn't get its fix. The body was still intact, but as long as the drug coursed through it, the soul would lie dormant. You would just be a human shell doing anything to keep getting fed the drug, including listening to whatever the possessor of it said to do."

"So the first stage was meant to signify how Giovanna felt when she and her lover were together," Rhonnie said, and Angelo nodded.

"And the second stage was meant to correlate the pain she had when they murdered him. Pure agony. Feeling like she would do anything to get him back," Ahli pitched in.

"Yes," Angelo said. "Soon, she had everyone hooked on the drug, and they were all doing her bidding. Looting, even killing for her. The darkness in her heart had erased all empathy, and the sweet girl she once was, was gone. Her tyranny spread to many other towns until finally, someone stopped her."

"Who?" Rhonnie asked in a low voice. She was into the story. "Who stopped her if they were all under her drug's spell?"

"Giovanna's husband. He was the only one who hadn't taken the *Vita E Morte*. He knew the only way to end the craze was to kill her and get rid of the drug forever, which he did. He also killed the witch, knowing she was the one making it. There was much chaos after, much like a withdrawal stage, but once their bodies were completely rid of *Vita E Morte,* they went back to their normal selves. Giovanna's husband, who was proclaimed town mayor after restoring balance, declared *Vita* a forbidden drug, and anyone caught trying to recreate it would be sentenced to death."

By the time he was done talking, the cigar in Angelo's fingers had gone completely out, and he looked like he was out of breath. The chills going up and down Ahli's body prevented her from speaking right away, but Rhonnie had a mouthful.

"So we're supposed to believe that those pills are some ancient hoodoo made by a woman scorned?" she asked with a disbelieving tone and expression. "And what, the witch was what we would call a scientist back in her time? Because the drug you're holding was made in a lab. Not in a witch's kettle."

"Of course the myth has been tampered with to make it into a good story to tell," Angelo told her, relighting his cigar. "I don't believe in witchcraft, but I do believe that even back then, they had enough information about the human body to create such a drug."

"So you believe that some of that story holds some truth to it? If that's the case, you believe that it was destroyed, right?" Ahli asked, finally finding her voice.

"I did not say that." Angelo took a drag from the cigar and blew out a huge puff of smoke. "I believe that even though the husband did not use it, he knew the formula. Tell me something that every great leader has just in case something threatens his rule and country?"

"Nuclear bombs," Rhonnie answered quickly.

"Exactly. I believe that Giovanna's husband kept one documented recipe of *Vita E Morte* and passed it down. Tell me something." Angelo held the bag of pills to eye level. "Has anyone taken any of these?"

"Yes," Ahli answered. "They had a few experimental subjects in our lab out of the States."

"And how long did that first high last, two days?" Angelo asked, and when they both nodded, he sighed. "Exactly. It's only a matter of time before the other stage sets in, and when it does, darkness will consume everything around us. This is a drug that should not be on this earth. You must destroy it."

"Wait, we haven't heard about any of the test subjects who took VEM or anyone else lashing out like zombies," Rhonnie told him. "Maybe what you're telling us is just a story."

"Maybe," Angelo gave the pills one last stare before tossing the bag to Ahli. "But you won't know until you see it for yourselves."

Rhonnie opened her mouth to make another retort, but Ahli grabbed her by the arm. She nodded at Angelo and gave him a forced smile.

"Thank you for your time. If we could, I would like to keep this meeting between us," Ahli said and then re-membered Jolanda. "And if you could tell your daughter not to say anything to Jaq, that would be great."

"I can if you promise me one thing."

"What's that?" she asked.

"That you'll do the right thing. And you have my word that my lips are sealed."

It was as if time around them stopped for the three seconds their eyes connected. His eyes said something that his lips didn't have to, and Ahli felt her head nodding. The moment he broke eye contact to take another drag of the cigar was the same one the sisters used to leave the study. They almost ran into Jolanda, who was carrying a plate of food back to Angelo.

"Leaving so soon?" Jolanda asked. "I made enough lasagna for everyone if you wanted to stay."

"No, thank you," Ahli spoke before Rhonnie could accept her offer. "We really should be heading back home. It's getting later by the second."

"All right," Jolanda said. "Did you find out whatever it was you needed to know?"

"Yes, we did," Ahli said as she and Rhonnie continued toward the foyer of the house. Before she closed the front door, she yelled over her shoulder, "Thank you!"

"I wanted some lasagna," Rhonnie pouted when they were safe and sound inside the car.

"We have bigger fish to fry."

"Yeah, say that when I'm starving, why don't you?"

"We can stop and get something to eat on our way to the hospital back at home."

"The hospital?" Rhonnie asked, making a face as she drove away from the house. "What's at the hospital?"

"Didn't you hear anything Angelo said?"

"All I heard was some crazy-ass story he told us."

"You're so annoying, but let me refresh your memory. He said we won't know until we see it for ourselves."

"Yeah, and?"

Ahli pulled out the bag of pills and shook them at her. "We need a test subject."

Chapter 8

Tina Swanson hadn't always been hooked on alcohol and drugs. In fact, she had a master's degree in education. She was on her way to becoming the superintendent of her school district and even engaged to marry the love of her life. However, when her son died in a terrible car accident, she just couldn't cope with the life around her anymore. Nothing mattered if she didn't have her boy to share her success with. She fell into a world of drug and alcohol abuse, and before she knew it, she looked up to see that twenty years had passed. She had lost everything: her man, her job, her house, her car, and now she was losing her health.

Her liver and kidneys were failing. There was nothing the doctors could do to stop it because she refused to give up her habits. The streets had dubbed her Crazy Tina because she had once scaled a building with the promise of a bag of cocaine and a fifth of any liquor she chose if she survived it. Well, she survived to tell the tale, but for how much longer was up in the air.

Ahli didn't know her very well, but a few of Sadie's runners did. At first, The Last Kings only served elite clients, but when her cousin Ray relocated, Sadie realized that fiends were going to be fiends, and they were going to find a way to get their high. So she opened the street market back up. Crazy Tina was always one of the first trying to get served when her social security check hit, so the dope boys knew her well.

Ahli knew she stayed in and out of the hospital due to health problems because Petey Boy was always talking about going to visit her. Ahli thought he'd been sweet on her once upon a time. After the talk with Angelo, she remembered that Petey Boy had said Crazy Tina was once again in the hospital. On the way back to Detroit, she called around to all the hospitals until she found the one the old woman was located in.

When they were back in Detroit, they ditched the Rolls-Royce for an unmarked Dodge caravan. They then stopped at a store and had a kid run in and buy the scrubs and nametags they had on when they got to the hospital. They parked in a parking lot across the street and away from any cameras.

"You do not look like an Amanda, by the way," Ahli told Rhonnie, glancing at the name her sister had chosen.

"And, bitch, you don't look like a Linette," Rhonnie snapped back at her. "You look like a Bobbie, since you be bobbing your head all over Brayland's—"

She was interrupted by Ahli's phone ringing. Ahli flinched at her like she was going to hit her, but she didn't. Instead, she looked at the phone screen and figured her sister had spoken him up, because it was Brayland calling.

"Hey, baby," she said.

"Don't 'hey, baby' me. Where the hell you been at?" he said, his voice coming through from the other end.

Even when he was agitated, his voice always sent flutters through her chest. She loved that man, and she hated that she was keeping secrets from him. Ahli hadn't told him any of what she and Rhonnie were doing, and she didn't plan to anytime soon.

"I'm sorry, Bray. I've just been trying to clear my head, that's all."

"Sadie said you and Rhonnie took off for a few days. She has me and another detail doing your job. Is everything good?"

"I'm good, baby, I promise," she said. "I don't want you to worry about me. Like I said, I'm just clearing my head to prepare for the mayhem VEM is going to bring."

"Tell me about it. Everybody who got the samples has already re-upped," he told her, and she almost stopped breathing.

"What? That fast?" she asked.

Rhonnie saw the look on her face and mouthed the words, "What's wrong?" Ahli held up a finger, telling her to wait a second.

"That's what I said. But yeah, even that nigga King Dex touched down to re-up. The only one who didn't is Cyril. The kid said something about people getting too hooked, but shit, I thought that was the goal. Anyways, you would know all this if you weren't out of the loop and shit."

"I'ma be back soon."

"You better be. I'ma let y'all get back to doing your sister thing, but I want you to know that I'm here for you, too, a'ight? I love you."

"I love you too," Ahli said in a bit of a hurry and disconnected the phone.

"What happened? Why do you look like that?" Rhonnie asked.

"Bray just told me that everyone has already re-upped on VEM," she said, looking into her sister's eyes.

"That was fast. Even Cyril?" she asked.

"No, Bray said he was the only one who didn't."

"I'm going to have to text him and see what's up," Rhonnie said absentmindedly and instantly realized her mistake.

"Text him?" Ahli furrowed her brow. "How the hell do you even have his number?"

"I was curious, okay?" Rhonnie said innocently. "I mean, he's cute, right? I sent him my number from my fake online profile, and yes, I told him it was me. He texted me, but I haven't texted him back. I guess with all this shit going on, I forgot about it."

"Well, yes, I'm going to need you to hit his line and see what's up with all this. He seems to be the only one with common sense."

"I will once we're done here. I can't believe you have me about to kidnap an old lady."

"You've done much worse."

"Touché."

Almost simultaneously, the girls checked the clips in their guns. Ahli didn't think they would have to use them, but then again, they could never be too careful. The two of them got out of the van and made the short hike to the hospital. They walked through the doors and adopted the same smiles as the workers around them. When they got to the door that only authorized personnel could get through, they pretended to look for their badges.

"You must be two of the newbies," a strong voice said from behind them.

Turning around, they saw a tall, sandy-haired white man standing there with a bright smile. He was wearing a white coat, letting them know he was a doctor, and he had a clipboard in his hands. He was handsome but had a stern look about his face as his eyes shifted from Ahli to Rhonnie.

"Uhh," Rhonnie said, almost blowing their cover, but Ahli had it covered.

"Yes, we forgot our badges at our apartment," she said with an innocent smile. "We were rushing to get to our shift. They're usually clipped to our scrubs, but I did laundry last night."

"No worries. I'll help you out this time. You can have Tom in HR make you some new ones for your shift tonight."

"Thank you, Doctor," Ahli said, batting her eyelashes, and he winked at her.

He used his badge to unlock the door, and Ahli was worried about him lingering over them. However, as soon as the door was open, he bustled through and left them in the dust.

"Flirting with the doctor, huh?" Rhonnie raised a brow, and Ahli smacked her lips.

"You act like you've never seen a movie a day in your life. Doctors always love trying to fuck the new interns. They'll do anything."

"Ooookay. Anyways, let's figure out what room Crazy Tina is in so we can get out of here."

"Already found that out when I called to see if she was here. Room 415, on the fourth floor."

"Let's go."

They maneuvered through the hospital, making sure to stay out of the way and off anyone's radar. They took an elevator up to the fourth floor and walked the halls until they located Crazy Tina's room. Ahli had hoped she would be asleep so that they could wheel her out in peace, but that's where their luck ended. Crazy Tina was wide awake in her hospital bed, flipping through channels on the television. The hair on her head was disheveled, and her face was sunken in like that of someone with a bad drug problem. When she saw them enter, her already-wide eyes grew wider in anger. She grabbed her tray of food and threw it at them, sending applesauce everywhere. Ahli ducked just in time, or else the tray would have hit her dead in the forehead.

"Get the fuck out!" she shouted in a hoarse voice. "I'm tired of you goddamn nurses coming in to check on me every ten minutes! I don't even want to be in this motherfucka, but that punk-ass doctor won't let me leave."

"Damn it, Crazy Tina. You got applesauce all on my new scrubs," Rhonnie exclaimed as if she were really upset. "We aren't nurses! We came to break you out."

"Break me out?" Crazy Tina perked up. "Well, why didn't you just say that, baby?"

She snatched out the needles that were in her arms and almost jumped from the bed. Rhonnie hurried to help her out of her hospital gown and back into her clothes and shoes while Ahli acted as the lookout.

"Hurry up, Rhonnie."

"I'm going as fast as I can."

"You two look familiar. Do y'all know Petey Boy?"

"Yeah, we're his nieces," Ahli lied.

"I knew that man loved me." Crazy Tina smiled. "Are y'all taking me to him?"

"Uhh . . ." said Ahli. She and Rhonnie shared a look. "Eventually. First, we're going to give you some of that stuff that you like."

"Even better! Hurry up and put my other shoe on, girl! I'm tryin'a get high!"

Once Rhonnie finally had the sneaker on Crazy Tina's foot, they grabbed a wheelchair that was in the corner of the room and made her sit down in it. Then Ahli grabbed the blanket that was on the hospital bed and put it over Crazy Tina and up to her shoulders to hide her clothes.

"Okay, Crazy Tina, I need you to pretend to be asleep, okay?"

"You ain't said nothing but a word, baby," she said.

Instantly Crazy Tina's head fell to her right shoulder, and her eyes closed as if she were knocked out asleep. Now it was time for the hard part: getting her out of there without being detected. Ahli opened the hospital room door and looked both ways before waving for Rhonnie to come on. They were able to make it down the elevator without running into anyone, but it was pushing the wheelchair to the back exit door of the hospital that proved to be challenging. There were nurses and doctors bustling all around them, and all it would take was one of them to see their patient in the clutches of two interns they'd never seen before.

"Shit." Ahli stopped in her tracks and grabbed Rhonnie's wrist to make her stop too.

They were almost home free when Ahli spotted the doctor with the sandy brown hair who had let them in. He was surrounded by a group of doctors, and they were all deep in discussion. She had a feeling that if they walked past, he would speak to them, and they couldn't afford the distraction. She looked around for a plan B and found it when her eyes fell on a door that led to a different exit.

"That way," she said and took off in that direction.

Rhonnie followed her, and once they were in the clear and the door was closed behind them, they got Crazy Tina to her feet. They hurried to get to the door with the big red EXIT on top of it. Once they were there, however, Crazy Tina tried to make her exit away from *them*.

"Hold on, wait a minute," Rhonnie said and snatched her back up.

"You can get the hell off me now! I'm free. I'm going home."

"You're coming with us," Rhonnie reminded her. "Remember, we have something you're going to like."

"And so does my usual dealer. Now get the hell off me!"

The sisters looked at each other, knowing that if Crazy Tina kept it up, she would draw unwanted attention. They tried to coax her, but she just got louder, so Ahli did the only thing she could think of. She pulled her gun out and put it to Crazy Tina's stomach.

"If you don't shut the fuck up, you're going to die right here and right now," she growled, and Crazy Tina instantly got quiet. "Good. Now when we open this door, you're going to stay quiet and walk casually with us to our vehicle across the street. Got it?"

She nodded quickly.

"Good. We're going to take you somewhere and give you some of our newest product."

"You want me to be a guinea pig?"

"Something like that."

"But what if I die?"

"You're dying anyway," Rhonnie told her. "This shit won't kill you, but if it does, at least you'll be going out the way you enjoy, right?"

Crazy Tina seemed to seriously be weighing her options, even though, in reality, she only had one. She looked down at Ahli's gun again before finally speaking.

"Okay, let's go."

***

They took Crazy Tina to one of Sadie's old stash houses. The front door creaked when they opened it, and a tart smell filled their nostrils when they entered. The shabby carpet throughout the house had a few stains on it, and all of the walls were white and bare. It was a house that Sadie hadn't used in a while because it had been raided a few years back. Nothing was found, but Sadie still held on to the property. It was still fully furnished, and everything inside it worked. However, you could tell by how dusty everything was that no one had been there in a while. *Good,* Ahli thought.

On the way there, they'd bought Crazy Tina some food, thinking that maybe she should have something in her stomach before she took the VEM. They took her to a bedroom inside the house, and she ate while sitting cross-legged on the old metal bed.

"I was starving!" Crazy Tina exclaimed as she scarfed down a burger and fries. "They weren't trying to give a bitch anything but soft food at that hospital. What was I gon' do with some applesauce?"

They waited patiently for her to get done with her food and strawberry soda, while listening to her complain about everything. When finally she was done, she looked at the girls and made a face.

"You bitches promised me drugs, so where's my shit at?"

"I'm only going to be so many more bitches," Rhonnie warned and reached in her pocket for the Baggie of pills. "Here."

"Just one?" Crazy Tina said when Rhonnie handed her the small white tablet.

"As you can see, there are more where that came from." Rhonnie rolled her eyes. "We just want to see the effect of one pill. We're told the high lasts for two days."

"Two days? As in two days straight?" Crazy Tina asked, and when the girls confirmed that with nods, she tossed the VEM back with no water. "I'll see you bitches when I come down!"

Ahli grabbed Rhonnie's arm and shook her head. The old woman was already a lost cause, so there didn't seem to be a point in beating her down for some words. She watched Crazy Tina as if expecting something to happen right away, but it didn't.

"I guess now we wait," she said with a sigh.

"Now we wait," Rhonnie repeated.

Chapter 9

"Another one, miss?" a bartender asked, approaching where Sadie sat alone at the bar.

She glanced at the empty glass in front of her. She hadn't even noticed that she'd downed the entire martini that fast. The only thing left was an olive on a toothpick, which she plucked out and ate.

"Yes, please," she said as she chewed and handed him her glass.

It had been a while since she decided to go out and have some time for herself. She just wanted a few moments of peace. She'd found some earlier when she stopped by Grandma Rae's home. Although the old woman wasn't there, Sadie swore she felt her spirit all around her whenever she walked through the doors. Maybe it was because her scent was still in the air, or the fact that Sadie often reflected on her fondest memories of her grandmother when she was in the home she'd grown up in. It was one of the things she had left of the woman who had raised her, and she cherished the place dearly. When she finally left and went home, she realized that she wasn't ready to stay home yet.

It had been Ahli telling her that Brayland had taken her dancing at Amor that reminded Sadie that she even owned the exquisite club. So that was where she ended up. She glanced around at the people sitting down eating and the couples on the dance floor. Before they greatly expanded, Amor had been the heart of The Last Kings' operation. Now the main purpose of Amor was to launder big amounts of money that she couldn't launder through her other businesses. She hadn't physically stepped foot inside in almost a year. It was also the first time in a while that Sadie had gone anywhere alone. However, that night, she decided to put on a beautiful black gown and enjoy some time to herself. She could have easily had someone else be her security for the evening since Rhonnie and Ahli were off doing whatever they were doing, but she didn't. She figured she could handle herself for an evening out. And if anything happened, she had a pistol in her Birkin to handle the problem.

There was a live band playing at Amor that night, and Sadie swayed to the melody as the singer on the stage sang her heart out. She had the kind of voice that sent chills up and down a person's spine. The bartender returned with her drink, and Sadie tipped him with a hundred-dollar bill.

"Thank you," he said and smiled bright, looking at the blue face.

"Anything for my employees," she said with a wink.

"Wait, y . . . you're the owner?" The lanky young black man was astonished.

"I am," she said and took a sip of her drink. "And you make the best martinis."

"Th . . . thank you," he said and looked frantically around at his area behind the bar. "It's a little untidy back here, but I'll get it together right away."

"No"—Sadie held a hand up and looked at his name-tag—"Brenton, don't worry about it. You're just fine. Keep doing your job like I'm not here."

He nodded, but Sadie could tell that he had grown nervous knowing that the owner of the club was there. He went out of his way to seem even more professional as he was helping other customers, and he even began obeying the rules as far as how much alcohol he was supposed to put in drinks. She was amused slightly as she watched him, and she wondered if she had looked so eager to please when she had tried to impress Ray in the beginning. She took another sip of the martini and was finally feeling a buzz coming on when somebody came up behind her.

"I almost wondered if you remembered this place existed."

That deep, sexy voice. It was one she used to yearn to hear daily, but now it only tormented her thoughts and dreams. It was Tyler's voice. Slowly, she placed her glass back on the bar top and turned around in her high seat. She didn't know what she would do if she saw him standing behind her with his fiancée, but judging by the way her heart stopped when she heard his voice, she wouldn't be able to handle it.

But no, he was alone and dressed in a nice black tailored suit. He towered over her, rocking a fresh lined-up cut, and she took notice that he'd removed most of his facial hair. The only thing that remained on his light-skinned face was a thin mustache that connected to a short beard. He looked better than ever, and happy. The aroma of the Tom Ford Fucking Fabulous cologne invaded her nostrils, and she fought to keep a satisfied moan from coming through her lips. It had been her favorite.

"Tyler," she said, and their eyes danced, but then she cleared her throat. "For a moment, I think I actually did forget about this place. Which is crazy, because it all started here."

"That it did," he said, and she watched him study her face as if trying to figure something out. "Can I join you for a moment?"

"Umm, sure?"

"You don't sound sure."

"No, no, I'm sorry." She shook her head. "Have a seat."

He did, and she instantly regretted it. Why had she done that? Just being in his vicinity was making her chest tighten.

"So how are you, Sadie?" he asked, turning the bar chair to face her. "I feel like we haven't spoken since—"

"I'm good," she interrupted him with the partial truth. "I'm sure you know that VEM is on the market now."

"I do. It's the only thing Ray has been talking about. They've already run out in Azua since they had to ship a large supply to us in the States."

"We'll be better prepared for the next batch," she said.

See, she could do it. Talk to him, that was. As long as they kept it about business, she would be fine. She could breathe.

"I'm sure we will. I've been meaning to tell you congratulations on that. Except we haven't talked since—"

"How are you, Tyler?" Sadie interrupted him again, and he gave her a knowing look but didn't press the fact.

"I've been good too. I haven't been in the streets too much since the engagement. I've been handling our business on the executive level now, like you. Making sure numbers match up, keeping the Feds off our back."

"How's Marie?" Sadie asked, referring to Tyler's younger sister, whose calls she'd also been avoiding.

"She's good. She would love to hear from you sometime. She said she's been trying to get in touch with you."

"I'll be sure to call her soon."

"Mm-hmm."

"Mm-hmm."

There was an awkward silence that came over them before Tyler suppressed a laugh. "Is this what we're going to do every time we see each other?" he asked.

"And what's that?"

"Pretend that we were never two people in love."

There it was. Sadie had spent so much time avoiding that very conversation that she hadn't prepared herself for it at all. It had crept up on her. She tried to look away, but her eyes went straight to his. It was electrifying, the chemistry between the two of them, and she felt it magnifying by the second.

"What do you want me to say, Tyler?" she asked in an exasperated tone.

"I don't know, something. Shit. I know you don't love me anymore, but you act like you can't stand me," he said, and the pain in his tone broke her heart

"If you want me to sit around and pretend like we are the best of friends, I can't," she told him.

"Why not? We used to be."

"That was before you proposed to another woman."

"You broke up with me!"

"I asked for space and time!" Sadie exclaimed. "I wanted to focus on VEM. But you were so selfish and bullheaded, you couldn't even put your pride aside to give me that."

"Bullshit. That's just the excuse you felt like using. You know, just like I know that you were never the same after Mocha died. It didn't matter how much love I gave you. I felt you pushing me away further and further every day."

"You've never talked to me about how I felt about Mocha."

"But I tried to! You just wouldn't open up to me like you used to when she was alive. I never would have given up on you, but it got to the point where it was like I couldn't make you happy anymore. And when you asked me for a break, I knew it was over. I've gone to war with many niggas, but when it came to the fight for our love? I couldn't win that by myself. You were mentally and emotionally detached from me before you even spoke the words. With Jada, things are just smoother. I don't have to fight, and I don't have to question her love for a nigga."

She tried to blink the tears away, but they still fell. The words he said were true. When Mocha died, Sadie lost a piece of herself forever. Even though she knew that Tyler would never do her the way Mocha had, it had been hard letting him touch the most intricate pieces of her. She was deeply and madly in love with him, but still, she couldn't figure out a way to give him all of her.

"You're right," she agreed, taking the rest of the martini to the head. She chuckled and wiped the tears away. "You deserve someone who can make you a happy man. Someone who can give you all of them. Not someone so fucked up, like me."

"Sadie, that's not what I—"

"You didn't have to say it, Tyler." She shrugged her shoulders. "You proposed to your fiancée in six months, which means she knocked you off your feet. Where is the future missus, anyways?"

"Right here," a pleasant voice said, walking up to them.

The voice belonged to a beautiful petite woman who looked to be the same age as Sadie. She, too, wore an elegant gown that went down to the floor and showed off her curvy frame. She wore her hair in a blunt-cut bob, and her face was beat to the gods. The engagement ring on her finger seemed to weigh her hand down, but that wasn't the only rock she sported. She wore a diamond necklace with the matching tennis bracelet, which stood out to Sadie partly because the pieces shined almost as brightly as her white teeth. Tyler's fiancée's eyes lit up when they fell on him.

"Baby, I've been looking all over this place for you," she said with a pout. "I came out of the bathroom and couldn't find you."

The two shared a passionate kiss in front of Sadie, giving her the sensation of someone wringing her throat and constricting her airflow. When they finally broke the kiss, the adoring look Tyler gave Jada made Sadie sick to her stomach. It was the way he used to look at her. That was *her* look. How dare he?

Tyler's fiancée finally remembered that someone else was over there with them and glanced at Sadie. Sadie watched a realization come over the woman, and the pleasant smile quickly faded from her lips.

"What's going on here, babe?" she asked Tyler suspiciously.

"Nothing, Jada. I just came to the bar to grab a drink, that's all," he said, kissing her hand. "I ran into Sadie. She owns Amor, remember?"

"Mmm," Jada said in a disapproving tone and turned her attention back to Sadie. "I was wondering when we would meet."

"Is that right?" Sadie said, cocking her head.

"Yes," Jada said, smiling big again and batting her eyelashes. "I guess I understand why he liked you. I mean, you're almost as pretty as me."

"He didn't like me. He loved me," Sadie corrected her. "And no need to be catty. I broke up with him, not the other way around. Isn't that right, Tyler?"

"Poor decision-making on your part," Jada shot back and placed a hand on Tyler's arm. "Only a fool would let something this great go."

"Maybe I am a fool, but you live and you learn. If something is meant, not even the strongest of minds can fend off the universe," Sadie said, and Tyler looked at her indifferently.

"There is no question there," Jada agreed. "When Tyler and I first met, I wasn't even thinking about a relationship. But he swept me off my feet, and I guess I have you to thank, Sadie. Tyler was a man with so much love to give, and he finally found someone to give it to. A real woman never shies away from something real. Tyler tells me all the time how nice it is being with someone who can be so appreciative and welcoming of his affections."

Sadie had to fight the sudden sensation she had to flick the olive in her glass at Jada's face. The way she kept saying her name was making her blood boil. She had taken more jabs than Sadie ever allowed without reacting, but still, Sadie held her composure. She knew that Jada was trying to get to her, and Sadie didn't want to show her emotions.

"Well, I'm glad Tyler finally found someone to be so . . . *open* with. I'm sure he's told you all about what he does for work."

"Yes, he's told me all about the many properties and businesses he owns all through Michigan. He's a very wealthy man."

"If that's all he told you, then you don't know him at all, honey," Sadie said and waved Brenton over to refill her glass. When he did, she took a sip and gave Jada a complete once-over. "I can see why that's all he told you. You don't look like you can handle the real story."

"Sadie," Tyler warned.

"I'm sorry, the liquor has me a little loose at the lips," she said and gave a fake giggle. "However, I do wish you both the best. I would ask what you want as your wedding gift. Maybe I should replace those diamonds." Sadie smiled and pointed at the jewels Jada sported.

"Oh, these? They don't need to be replaced," Jada bragged, extending her arm to give Sadie a closer look at the diamond bracelet. "Tyler got them for me. It's—"

"A seven-inch platinum bracelet with a box catch and princess-cut diamonds," Sadie finished.

Jada looked taken aback and retracted her wrist. Her smile wavered but didn't leave her pretty face, and she gave a giggle. Next to her, Tyler began to fidget in his seat, but she didn't notice.

"Oh, you must have the same one," Jada said.

"I did, actually. I left them at Tyler's and just haven't gone back to get them. As a matter of fact, your necklace looks just like the diamond necklace I left over there, too." Sadie made a "tsk" sound with her tongue and continued in a sarcastic tone. "Tyler, is your fiancée wearing my jewelry?"

"I didn't think you wanted them," Tyler said after being put in the hot seat and having two sets of eyes on him. "I called you to come get the rest of your things, but you never wanted to talk about anything but business."

"They're still mine. Thank you so much, Jada, for bringing them to me," Sadie said coldly and extended her hand as if to tell Jada to take her jewelry off.

Jada gave a small laugh as if what Sadie was insinuating was ridiculous, but Sadie was dead serious. Sadie knew she was being childish, but she didn't care. Jada already had the love of her life. She wouldn't be leaving there with her diamonds, too. Her hand inched toward her purse, which was on the bar top. If Jada wasn't going to give her the diamonds willingly, Sadie was prepared to whip her with the pistol in her Birkin. The motion didn't go unnoticed by Tyler, and he stood between the women.

"Chill out, Say," Tyler said with a stern voice and hardened expression. She felt her heart break even more because she'd never seen him stare so coldly at her.

"Nigga, you regifted this bitch my diamonds, and you expect me to chill out?" Sadie stood as well.

"Who are you calling a bitch?" Jada squealed from behind Tyler, clearly not knowing who she was dealing with. "I'm not giving you shit. You're just a bitter ex, mad because I have what you want."

"Tyler, tell this *bitch* I will murder her," Sadie said, and Jada laughed, thinking it was an idle threat. Tyler knew better, though.

"You're not going to hurt my fiancée, and she's not taking anything off," he said, angered by Sadie's threat. "I never thought you could be so childish. My future wife and I came to have a nice evening out, and that's what we're going to do. If you want, I'll wire the cost of the jewels to your account in the morning."

Sadie knew that if she didn't get out of there, she would do something she would later regret. His words stung so much that she felt tears welling up in her eyes again. His "fiancée." His "future wife." He had made sure to throw those words in her face. Before she left, the alcohol coursing through her system was giving her the courage to do one more thing: tell him how she really felt. She took a step back and glared at Tyler from his shoes all the way back up to his face. When she got to his eyes, her glare subsided and was replaced with a look of deep sadness.

"You know what? You were right about me," she said, laughing in spite of herself. "I did push you away. I pushed you away for something I thought could never turn on or hurt me: my work. The closer you and I got to doing the forever thing, the more I felt like I couldn't breathe. I thought it was because I wasn't ready, but it was because I was terrified. My entire life has been a gamble, and what made you so different? But you were different. You were always different. You had me since that first trip to Jamaica, and you never let me go until I made you. And for that, I'm sorry."

"Sadie—" Tyler's expression softened.

"I'm not finished," she said and looked him in the eyes, letting a single tear roll down her cheek. "I thought . . . I thought I would be okay, you know? Seeing you move on and be happy. But I never stopped loving you, Tyler, and I don't know if I ever will. If I had known that you were going to give another woman the life we built for us, I would have tried a little harder to let you in. But that's in the past now. And after this, we have no other reason to speak. I'll be checking my account for the money for those diamonds."

She didn't say goodbye. She just snatched up her bag and walked away from the bar without looking back. She was afraid that if she did, she wouldn't be able to leave. Her legs felt like Jell-O with each step she took, and a part of her was hoping that Tyler would run after her. But by the time she was inside of her gray Ferrari 488 Spider, she let go of that thought. She was upset and tipsy, which meant she really shouldn't have been driving. But she didn't care. It wouldn't be her first time driving under the influence.

"It's okay. It's okay," she told herself as she pulled out of Amor's parking lot. Her throat was tight like she'd swallowed a golf ball, and she fought back the urge to cry. "All things come to an end."

Chapter 10

Making it home in one piece seemed to be the only good thing that happened that night. When Sadie walked into the house from the garage, she had to hold the wall to keep from stumbling into collapse. Not because of the liquor, but because she'd finally gotten her closure, and it wasn't the good kind. She and Tyler were really over. Although she'd said it aloud numerous times, the truth now finally stared her in the face.

By the time she made it to the kitchen, she was a complete mess. She was glad that Rhonnie and Ahli weren't there to see her in such shape. Her vision was blurred by the drops of water in her eyes, and the only thing she could think to do was throw her purse into a wall. She heard the Birkin crash into it, and she had to admit the little release of frustration felt good, so she kept going. Anything that was in her grasp got thrown into the walls around her: plates, glasses, appliances, anything she could pick up. The only thing that could be heard was the shattering of her own property echoing on the high ceilings.

"I don't want it!" she screamed and threw two wine glasses at the sink. "I don't want any of it!"

When finally she had exhausted all of her energy, she dropped to the ground. The skirt of her gown flowed around her like a pool of blackness, just like her heart.

Empty. Her lips quivered as regret ate away at her subconscious. She had a mansion, more cars than anyone needed, and so much money that her legacy would be wealthy for years to come. But none of that meant anything without love. There was no point in having the world with no one to share it with. Sadie closed her eyes and hung her head in shame. What had she done?

"I'm sorry," she whispered tearfully. "I'm so sorry, Tyler."

"Sorry for what?"

"For being too proud to let you know that I need you," Sadie said aloud to Tyler's voice in her head.

"You need me?"

"Yes, but now it's too late. I'll never get you back."

"Sadie?"

She ignored his voice. She'd had enough of it plaguing her mind.

"Sadie?"

"Leave me alone!" she shouted. "Please just get out of my head."

"I'm not in your head. I'm right here."

She felt someone grab her hands in front of her, and she opened her eyes. There Tyler was kneeling right in front of her. It hadn't been the voice in her head talking to her. It had been him. She wondered if she had conjured up his image like she had conjured up his voice. She almost didn't believe it, but she could feel him and knew it was true.

"T . . . Tyler?" Sadie asked with a befuddled expression. "What are you doing here? How did you get in?"

"After you left, I just didn't feel like I was in the right place anymore," he told her, wiping away her tears. "And I got in because I've never thrown away my key."

"I told the guards to not let you in anymore," Sadie told him.

"You think them niggas could really stop me from getting in here?" he asked, making a face. "Plus, I helped design and pay for this place."

"I can't believe you brought your fiancée to our house. Where is she at, in the car?"

"I left her."

"Then you better go outside to her. I don't have time for her coming in here looking for you. I might kill her for real."

"No, Sadie." Tyler reached in the jacket of his suit and brandished the diamond necklace and bracelet Jada had been wearing. "I *left* her."

"You mean, *left her* left her?" Sadie asked, troubled. "But why? I thought . . . I thought you loved her."

"I did too," he sighed and shook his head. "But after seeing you tonight, and after the things you said, I realized that I was just projecting all the love I had for you onto her. I *am* ready to do the forever thing, but I had the wrong leading lady."

"Tyler . . ."

"Listen, Say, I love you too. I love you to the moon and back more times than I'll ever live to count. With Jada, I was just a shell of myself. I thought I was happy, but when I saw you sitting at the bar alone, I had to face just how sad I really was. A nigga been lost without you. Why do you think I'm here? Being that close to you again, it felt like gravity was pulling me to you or something."

"But the way you looked at her . . . and you have her all over social media. You didn't even do that with *me*."

"I was trying to make you jealous because you were acting so heartless. I felt like I needed to make you see me, but I saw that I only hurt you more. And it made me feel like shit. And you being hurt has always been the problem. You've been hurting this entire time, and I always made shit about me. I see why you pushed me away."

"Tyler, you don't have to blame yourself. Everything is my fault."

"And it's my fault too. I'm so used to you being tough, I don't remember the last time you were so wide open with me. I needed that, more than you could ever know. I needed to know . . . I needed to know that you still loved me. I don't want to go through life without you, ma. Half a year already felt like a lifetime."

"You had someone keeping you warm, though," Sadie told him. "I can't believe you proposed to her."

"I called off the wedding."

"When?"

"Right after you left. My face still hurts from the slap Jada gave me," Tyler said, rotating his jaw.

"Serves you right." Sadie felt a smile coming to her lips.

"Shit, I'll take a slap to the face over what the walls of this place had to endure," he said, looking around the kitchen with wide eyes. "Sheesh, woman. I'm glad I showed up *after* the tornado hit this motherfucka."

"Still a comedian, I see," she said with a sniffle.

"Ain't this the part when we kiss?" Tyler asked in a hopeful voice, but Sadie made a face.

"I'm not kissing you until you give me my money for those diamonds," she said, and when he looked at her incredulously, she rolled her neck. "I'm dead-ass serious. I don't care if you brought them back, Ty. You had my shit all on that bitch's neck and arm. I don't want them."

"You made that whole fuss—"

"Because she had my nigga! I didn't care about them diamonds."

"Had, right?"

"Yes," Sadie said and couldn't contain the urge anymore. She snatched her hands from his and threw her arms around his neck, holding him tight like she'd been yearning to. "Had, because I'm never letting you go again."

He hugged her back and held her as if he were afraid she would disappear. They embraced for so long that Sadie's arms began to quiver, but she didn't care. She was happy. Behind his back, she pinched herself just to make sure she really wasn't hallucinating. When she felt the pain, she pulled back and admired his face. Although she had told him that she didn't want to kiss him, her lips had a mind of their own. They pressed on his softly, and he returned her kiss of passion. She slipped her tongue in his mouth, and when it met his, they did a dance of love. The fervent kiss turned into their hands exploring each other's bodies and then to them being naked on the kitchen floor.

Sadie hadn't been intimate since the last time they were together, so the place between her legs was hot and ready. She was so wet that she felt her juices sliding down the crack of her ass as she lay on the cold kitchen floor. She wanted to feel him inside of her, but Tyler was taking his time and giving each inch of her attention. She squirmed and writhed as his tongue worked wonders on her ears and neck, while his hands fondled her breasts.

"Hsss," she hissed when he bit her earlobe at the same time that he pinched her nipples. Her back arched, and she moaned out loud, "I love you, Tyler."

He didn't respond with words. Instead, he showed her. He began to suck her nipples, and in between switching breasts, he mushed his face with them. His manhood was rock hard against her leg, and she had to admire his restraint. Sadie could tell by the rigid way he breathed that he was dying to dive inside of her. He had always been that way, wanting to please her and suffer in the process. She wouldn't allow it anymore.

In a sudden motion, she pushed him off her and flipped him on his back. He lifted his head to see what was wrong but was met with her fat cat and round cheeks in his face. She wanted him to pleasure her while she pleasured him.

"Don't drown," she said, looking sexily back at him as she wrapped her petite hand around his shaft.

"Don't choke," he told her right before gripping her thighs and flicking his tongue on her clit.

The electrifying feeling almost made her jump, but he had too firm of a grip on her legs for her to go too far. The only thing that could stop her from shouting out in pleasure was putting his dick in her mouth. The feel of its tip hitting the back of her throat and its veins on her tongue turned her on. Her mouth was filled with saliva, and it dripped on his pubic hair as she gave him head. She sucked, licked, and spit all over it until she saw his toes curl. She was just trying to keep up with him, because the sensation between her legs was pure heaven. She hurried to push her orgasm out, because she knew Tyler like the back of her hand. If she got him to cum from head, he would be knocked out for the rest of the night, and she needed to feel his meat inside of her before that happened.

"Oh, shit," she breathed, taking his manhood from her mouth and jacking it off. "Oh, daddy. Yessss!"

"Cum in my mouth," he instructed. "Stroke on daddy's dick and cum in my mouth."

And she did just that. Her body shook like crazy when her clit exploded in a fit of bliss. He smacked her thighs, making her bottom jiggle before pushing her gently off his face. Without giving her time to recuperate from her first orgasm, Tyler bent Sadie over and arched her back as deep as it could go.

"Goddamn, I missed this ass and this pretty-ass pussy," he said, sliding his thumb up her cat's wet slit right before shoving it in her ass. "You gave my pussy away?"

"Nooo!" Sadie cried and clenched her vaginal walls while he finger fucked her anus.

"You swear?"

"Yes," she promised.

A part of her wanted to curse him out for the nerve of his question. He had slept with someone else, so how could he be such a hypocrite? But she was so horny, she didn't care. All that mattered was that he was back, and no other woman would ever sample what was created for her.

"Good," he said, positioning his tip at her opening and gripping her hip with his free hand. "I'm about to tear this pussy up."

Sadie choked on air when he plunged deep inside of her love canal. He thrust in and out of her with his prodigious third leg while still working magic with his thumb. She felt her head twisting left and right as she bared her teeth and bit down on her lip. It felt so good, too good in fact, and she almost wasn't able to take it. Bringing her to a second orgasm was almost too easy for Tyler. He knew her body like he had studied it for a test.

"Turn over. I need to see your face," he instructed and flipped her on her back.

That time, before he inserted himself inside of her, he stared affectionately down at her. The love he had for her radiated off his body, and she knew he could feel the same coming from her. She reached a tremulous hand up and caressed his sweaty face tenderly. There was so much that she could say, so much that she should say, but their bodies were already having the conversation. Their lips met again, and Sadie wrapped her legs around his waist. He released the hold he had on his lower body and fell into her. Her fingers scratched his back the moment his tip touched her cervix, but she didn't tell him to stop. The pain felt so good, and she tightened around his shaft with each stroke. For a while, the only sound that could be heard in the destroyed kitchen was them kissing sloppily and his balls slapping against her skin.

"Shit!" Tyler exclaimed, breaking their kiss.

One of his eyes was lower than the other, but they were both rolling. Sadie knew that he was almost to his climax, and so was she. She matched him thrust for thrust until they both shouted in unison. Sadie's vaginal walls pulsated while his manhood throbbed inside of her, releasing all of the cum in his balls. Out of breath, the two of them just lay there on the kitchen floor as one. When he tried to move, she held on to him so that he couldn't. She wasn't ready for him to. Not yet. She had just gotten him back. She didn't want him to leave and go to wherever his new home was. She wanted him to stay with her in the house they'd built together.

"Stay," she whispered in his ear.

"I'm not going anywhere tonight," he spoke in a voice that let her know he had barely any energy left.

"No, I mean . . . forever. Come back."

He partially lifted up to look into her eyes as if to see if she was being serious. "You mean move back in?"

"That's exactly what I mean."

"Are you sure? I don't want you to feel like you have to say that just because I just gave you the best dick of your life."

"You're such an idiot!" Sadie found herself laughing. "Besides that fact, I'm serious. I want you back. I want you home. Everywhere I look in this place, I see you. So it just makes sense that you're here."

"Okay," he said, smiling big.

"But I still want my money for those diamonds."

The next morning, Sadie still hadn't heard from Rhonnie or Ahli, and her curiosity had risen. To be truthful, if it hadn't been for Tyler being back, she probably would have called to check in. However, she was so elated to have her man that, after a while, the girls were just an afterthought.

Tyler had helped her put the kitchen back in order and, as promised, wired over the money for the diamonds. Anyone else might have been concerned that just the day before, he was an engaged man, but Sadie had lived through much more bizarre happenings than that. She and Tyler were soulmates. She knew that deep down. No matter where either one of them went, they would always yearn for one another. Which was why it just made sense that they be together. She was willing to put the past in the past and move forward. Everything was coming together. She had Tyler, everyone had re-upped on their supply of VEM, and not only that, but Tyler told her over breakfast how the streets were buzzing.

"I'm proud of you, Say," he said to her while scarfing down his scrambled eggs. "I've never seen anything like it. This shit is really like a new epidemic."

"I tried to tell you that I was on to something." She waved her fork at him. "I knew it the moment Ray sent me the results from our test patients. If it weren't for Ahli giving me the formula, though, none of it would have been possible."

"Speaking of her, where is Ahli and that crazy-ass sister of hers?"

"I gave them some time off," Sadie said simply.

"That explains why you were alone last night. You still need to bring someone with you," he chastised her. "How are they doing, though?"

"Good, but I think Ahli is having some second thoughts."

"About VEM?"

"Yeah." Sadie thought back to the moment she had told Ahli that the drug was ready. "She wasn't very happy when I told her VEM was ready to be sold in the States. And when she found out it's already being sold in Azua, there was unmistakable regret across her face."

"Do you think she regrets giving you the drug, or choosing to work for you?"

"They both go hand in hand," Sadie told him.

"So then, you're questioning her loyalty to you?"

"Yes," Sadie said but then shook her head. "I mean, no. There just is something off about how she's been acting these past days, that's all. I asked Rhonnie to keep an eye on her."

Tyler laughed and almost spit out his juice. Sadie looked at him as if he were crazy and tried to figure out what was so funny.

"You asked her sister, aka her best friend in the whole world, to keep an eye on her."

"Exactly."

"And you think she's not going to tell her?"

"I'm counting on it."

"I'm confused." Tyler wrinkled his brow.

"If Ahli knows I want her watched, her truest self will show. I'm sure that whatever they are doing has something to do with that."

"And that doesn't bother you?"

"No. Ahli needs to see on her own that VEM has the qualities of being the best drug ever created. The sooner, the better."

Tyler opened his mouth to talk, but his phone rang. Sadie was sure that it wasn't Jada because Tyler answered on the first ring.

"What's up, bro?" he said. "Nah, it's not a bad time. Word? I thought everything was going good. Damn. Nah, there ain't even a need to do all that. She's sitting right here. Hold on."

Tyler handed Sadie the phone, and when she looked at the caller ID, she smiled.

"Hi, cousin," she said into the phone and waited to hear Ray's cheery voice talk back to her.

"Sadie," he started, but his voice wasn't cheery or pleasant at all. "We need to talk. There is something that you need to see."

Chapter 11

Four days later, Brayland walked down a dark alley toward where his car was parked. It was a little after ten o'clock, and he had just finished doing a quick drop-off. When he was almost to his car, he heard a rustling behind him, and he turned to see what it was. Not too far behind him, there were what looked to be three fiends: two women and a man. They looked at him with wide eyes and sunken faces, and they had several teeth missing. They moved closer to him, and Brayland sighed, preparing to tell them to get on. It wasn't unusual for fiends to be pushy when they begged for drugs, but there was nothing free in life. If they didn't have the bread, they couldn't get served.

"What y'all looking for?" Brayland asked.

"VEM," one of the women said in a raspy voice.

"I don't have any on me," Brayland lied. He actually had a few Baggies full in his bag, but at $100 a pop, he doubted any of them had it to pay. Even if they put all their coins together, there was no way they could share one pill.

"Liar!" the man shouted. "Open your bag."

"Nigga, you tripping." Brayland almost laughed.

"I said, open that bag!" the man exclaimed and took off toward Brayland with a look of savagery.

Brayland didn't even bat an eye. He brandished his pistol from its holster and aimed it at the man barreling toward him. He thought that by seeing the weapon, the man would stop, but he didn't. In fact, suddenly, the other two began running toward him too.

"VEM! VEM! VEM!" they shouted repeatedly while they ran.

He didn't have a choice. Brayland let three shots off. The two women dropped dead instantly from head shots, but the man acted as if the bullet to the chest didn't hurt him at all. Brayland fired two more times, hitting the man in the leg and neck. He jerked from the impacts of the bullets, but he still kept coming.

"I don't know what kind of superman shit you're doped up on, but you need to die already!"

"VEM!" the man shouted again right before Brayland shot one last bullet that caught him in the forehead.

That time the fiend dropped to the ground. Their blood spilled onto the pavement in the alley, and Brayland knew it was time to get out of there. He got in his vehicle and drove off without looking back. However, what had just happened replayed over and over in his mind. He could tell by the looks in their eyes that the fiends were already high off something. Could it have been VEM? Brayland had never seen someone take three bullets and that person not be affected by the shots. Well, until that night.

It was still fresh on his mind when he heard his phone start ringing from the armrest. He glanced quickly from the road to grab it and see who it was before answering.

"Baby, the weirdest shit just happened to me," he started when he picked up.

"Brayland, I need you to get over here right now," Ahli told him in an urgent tone.

"Is everything all right?" he asked, instantly forgetting about the fiend. "Are you good?"

"Please, can you just get here? I don't know who else to call."

"Where are you?"

"At the old stash spot. The one that got raided a while back."

"Why are you there?"

"I'll explain when you get here. Can you come or not?"

"I'm on my way," Brayland said. "I'm about thirty minutes out."

"Okay. And, Bray?"

"Yeah?"

"Don't tell anyone where you're going, okay? Especially Sadie."

"Do I even want to be involved in whatever it is you're doing?"

"Brayland!"

"Okay, okay. But you don't have to worry about me telling her. She left for Azua a few days ago with Tyler."

"Azua? With *Tyler*?"

"Once again, if you were around, you would know all this," Brayland told her. "But I'ma see you in a second."

He disconnected the call and changed his route. The highway was clear that night, so he actually made it to the stash spot in twenty minutes. When he got there, he took notice of Rhonnie's Rolls-Royce parked outside. As he walked to the door of the old house, he hoped everything was okay. All the lights in the front were off, and if it hadn't been for the car and the fact that Ahli told him she was there, he wouldn't have thought anybody was home. The door opened before he could knock, and Ahli stood there in a pair of jeans and a loose T-shirt.

"Well, I'm here," he said, raising his hands after entering the house. "What was so important?"

Ahli didn't answer right away. She poked her head outside and looked up and down the street before shutting the door and locking it. After it was secure, she grabbed his hand and took him toward the back room.

"Before you see what I've really been up to for the last three days, I want to say don't be mad at me."

"Yeah, because that's the best way to start a sentence."

"For real, Bray, this is serious."

"Okay, what did you do?"

"Rhonnie and I dressed up as interns and broke Crazy Tina out of the hospital the other night."

"You did what?" Brayland asked and snatched his hand away from her, stopping in the hallway. "Why would you do that?"

"Because we needed a test patient," Ahli told him simply.

"A test patient for what exactly?"

"For VEM. I just didn't have a good feeling at all about it, and well, I was right. Come see."

She continued to the bedroom in the back, and Brayland waited a few moments before following her. Rhonnie was in the bedroom sitting on a chair in the corner, and she nodded at him when she saw him. He turned his attention to the bed and saw Crazy Tina lying there looking at the ceiling. Her eyes were glossy, and her skin seemed unusually dry, almost pale. His eyes trailed up her arms, and he noticed that both of her wrists had been tied tightly to the bedposts. Her lips were moving, and she was whispering something. The closer he looked, he saw that she was saying the same word over and over.

"*VEM.*"

His eyes widened, thinking back to the fiends in the alley, and he turned his attention back to Ahli. "What's wrong with her?"

"We gave her a few doses of VEM," Ahli answered him. "At first, she was just like those people in the video. Happy and high. Normal. But now—"

"She's like this," said Rhonnie.

"Why do you have her tied up like that?" Brayland asked, and the sisters exchanged a look. "Why y'all looking like that?"

"She's not the same," Ahli tried to explain.

"She looks like the same Tina I've always known, except"—Brayland took a step toward the bed and focused on Crazy Tina's face—"her eyes. There's something different about her eyes. They're darker."

"The VEM changed her," Ahli said. "She got addicted to it almost instantly, and now she's like this."

"And that's not all. Watch," Rhonnie said and turned to Crazy Tina. "Tina, you want some VEM?"

"VEM!" Crazy Tina's body jerked up fast, and she eyed the room hungrily. "Give me VEM now!"

She began fighting against her restraints so ferociously that the bed rocked back and forth. She bared her teeth, and the veins on the sides of her neck popped out. The legs of the bed lifted off the ground. Brayland was shocked because he didn't know a woman in her condition could have so much strength.

"Whoa," he said with growing eyes. "She's strong."

"It's the VEM," Ahli told him. "We had to tie her up because she punched a hole through the wall." She pointed at one of the bedroom walls, and there indeed was a hole the size of a small fist in it.

"The only thing she keeps asking for is more VEM. I think she would do anything for it," Rhonnie said. "We're trying to give her body time for the drug to run its course before we let her free."

"You know, before you called, I just had the strangest run-in with three fiends," Brayland said, never taking his eyes off Crazy Tina. "They were doing the same thing. They even tried to get at me. I had to put them down, but . . ."

"But what?"

"The man. I put three bullets in him, and he acted like they didn't even hurt him. He didn't stop coming until I put a bullet in his brain. You think they were high on VEM? Do you think the drug is giving them strength like that?"

"It's a good possibility," Ahli said with a sigh, staring at Crazy Tina, who was looking back at the three of them with wide and empty eyes. "I think it's safe to say that *Vita E Morte* was locked away for a reason. We don't need a whole bunch of souped-up people walking around like this. It's too dangerous. VEM needs to be destroyed."

Chapter 12

New Mexico

"Madame, we have someone here to see you."

Olivette Jenkins had been sitting at her desk and tapping a pen on her lips when the man's voice sounded. She had been staring out the window, and even with the new presence, her eyes never left the gardener trimming the bushes in the front yard of her seven-bedroom, four-bathroom home. After a few moments of no reaction from her, the man cleared his throat as if to remind her of his presence. Annoyed at his nerve, Olivette reached for one of two sharp spike sticks in the bun on the back of her head and threw it swiftly toward him without looking. She heard the man jump in fear for his life right before the impact as the stick hit its target.

"A few inches to the left and that would have been in your throat, Jeffrey," she said, finally shifting her eyes from the window. She saw Jeffrey, a hired hand who worked strictly for her, looking shaken at the spike stick lodged in the open door next to him. "Don't ever clear your throat at me again. Don't you think that's rude?"

"I . . . I was just trying to get your attention, madame. To inform you that your guest has arrived," Jeffrey stated and swallowed the lump in his throat.

"Well, why are you still here looking like a puppy that can't obey his master? Send him in."

Jeffrey was a muscular man with blond hair who stood just over six feet tall, but he seemed to be petrified of Olivette, who was easily five feet, five inches tall. Maybe it was the chill in that gaze of her auburn-colored eyes or the cold feel of the air that swirled around them. Or maybe it was because he had seen firsthand the merciless things she could do. Whichever it was, Jeffrey didn't wait to be told again what to do. He quickly glanced at the spike stick in the door before making a beeline to retrieve Olivette's guest. She smirked to herself before getting up from the black leather Timko executive desk chair. Humming a made-up tune to herself, she retrieved her hair accessory and made a mental note to have the door replaced.

Olivette fed on the fear of everyone around her. It was how she thrived. For her, fear and wealth brought loyalty. Her father, Oliver Jenkins, lucked out in his youth when he bought land that was right above an unclaimed oil line in Texas. It had been where he and his wife, Sharon, a black woman, had planned to build their home and start their family. However, with the turn of events, he decided to build his oil company on top of it instead. He was a millionaire within a year of the business being open.

The only thing he ever wanted in life was to have a child. His family didn't approve of his marriage to a black woman and warned him about the woes of bringing a mixed-race child into the world, but he didn't care. He loved Sharon and wanted a family of his own. Little did he know, the daughter they birthed would be the reason for the greatest joy he ever felt, but also his biggest regret.

Olivette's smirk turned into a full-blown smile when she sat back down at her desk. She rolled the spike stick between her fingers as she reflected on her dear, sweet father.

"But, Daddy!" 17-year-old Olivette whined with tears in her eyes. "I want to go to Spelman! It's a great college!"

"Olivette, I will not pay for you to go to a school just so you can gallivant around and have fun," Oliver Jenkins stated calmly. "College is something to take seriously."

"Honey, listen to your father," Sharon told her daughter.

The three of them were seated around the dinner table, enjoying what was supposed to be a harmonious meal. Olivette was still in her work uniform, and her father was still dressed in his work suit. Sharon, a stay-at-home mom, was the best cook, and that night she had whipped up her famous roast and potatoes. It was Olivette's favorite, but she was having a hard time stomaching it. She would be leaving for college the next year and had gotten into every school she'd applied for, including Harvard, which was where her father wanted her to attend. Olivette had different plans for her future and wanted to go to Spelman. She had finally worked up the nerve to tell her father that, but he laughed at the thought of her attending an HBCU.

"But, Daddy—"

"I said no, Olivette! And that is final. You will attend Harvard like we've previously discussed."

Olivette glared into his auburn eyes, the same ones she had, and felt a dangerous rage well up in her stomach. She always had a nasty temper about her ever since she was a little girl. Her parents blamed it on the fact that she was bullied often as a child. The Jenkins fam-

ily lived in a neighborhood that didn't see many people with brown skin, so the neighborhood kids were cruel to Olivette. They wouldn't play with her, because although she had a fair complexion and her hair was long, it was "kinky" just like "nigger" hair. Her parents would just tell her to give them time, but there wasn't enough time in the world.

It wasn't until she accidently killed the family cat that they knew she needed help. After that, they forced her to see a therapist three times a week. The therapist prescribed her pills that calmed her so she wouldn't have as many outbursts. Little did they know, she stopped taking them her senior year of high school. It had just been to loosen up, but the truth was, she liked herself better when she didn't take them. When she was on the medication, it made her feel as if her true self were locked in a room with padded walls. It was a fact that the medicine helped with her anger, but it also suffocated her other feelings. Olivette thought she could just control her emotions if she ever got mad. However, as she sat there, looking into her father's stern face, the anger she felt was uncontrollable.

"Why?" she pressed. "Why can't I just go to Spelman? Is it because it's a black school?"

"Yes," Oliver answered honestly and without remorse. "Yes, it is."

"Well, news flash: I'm black!"

"Half black," he corrected.

"It's all the same. One drop of black blood makes me a minority," Olivette reminded him and looked at her mother. "Are you seriously going to let him make me go to a school I don't want to?"

"He's paying for it, dear," Sharon said.

"'He's paying for it, dear,'" Olivette mocked, and Sharon looked taken aback. "God! You sound just like one of these white women! Look at your skin. Another news flash: you're black too! Or did you forget that since you're married to a wealthy white man? Fucking sellout."

"Now, I will not stand for you to talk to your mother that way!"

"And I won't stand for you to tell me what I'm going to do with my life," Olivette shouted back and jumped to her feet. "You already made me go to that snooty-ass private school with kids who hate me!"

"Don't be ridiculous. They don't hate you, Olivette," Sharon said in a tone suggesting that she was being silly.

"The only reason they tolerate me is because my dad is richer than their dads. Every time I look up, I'm swiping my card for something they want. I don't want it to be like that in my college years. I want to be around people who like me for me. Don't you get that?" Olivette pleaded with her father.

"I'm sorry, Olivette," Sharon said, but Olivette didn't feel like she was sorry at all.

"Let me ask you something, Mom. What's my favorite color?"

"It's purple," Sharon answered and made a face as if it were an easy answer.

"Wrong," Olivette told her. "Dad, what's my favorite movie? My favorite thing to do?"

"Olivette. You're being ridiculous," he sighed.

"Just say that you don't know." Olivette stepped back from the table and shook her head at them. "You two don't know anything about me. You're not even interested in me. You just want to control me and turn me into a

version of the daughter you have in your heads. And it won't happen!"

"All this over a decision we made months ago?" Oliver asked, exasperated. "Regardless of how unethical it might be, Harvard will always look better on an application than Spelman. Those are just the cold, hard facts. I don't care about this sudden 'black girl magic' kick you've been on, and quite frankly, nobody does. You're going to Harvard."

"You can't control my life!"

"The hell I can't."

"Then I'll just leave," Olivette challenged.

"Be my guest," Oliver said and gestured toward the door of the spacious home. "But you better call a taxi, because the BMW I bought you for your birthday is going to stay parked where it is."

"Honey, she won't be able to call a taxi, because she won't have any money after I cancel her credit cards," Sharon chimed in.

The two of them looked at each other and shared a hearty laugh at Olivette's expense. She watched the two of them and could see that they were truly enjoying the moment. Olivette's ears began to ring, and for a second, she forgot where she was. She looked down at the half-eaten food on the table and swiped it across the room. It crashed loudly into the wall, and gravy got everywhere, but she didn't care.

"You're going to regret this," she warned and marched out of the room.

"'You're going to regret this,'" Oliver mocked in between his laughter. "What's she gonna do, kill us?"

Little did he know that was exactly what she would do. Later that night, something terrible happened, leaving

Olivette parentless. The police and detectives deemed the fire that killed Oliver and Sharon Jenkins a freak accident caused by bad wiring in the house. They told Olivette how lucky she was to have been out grabbing a pizza from the gas station when it all took place. She turned 18 the next month and inherited all of the Jenkinses' millions, not to mention the insurance from the house fire.

Olivette had never felt that kind of freedom before in life. There was no remorse in her heart, only joy. She could do whatever she wanted to do, and the decision she made was to not go to college at all. She refused to be told what to do ever again. So she became a boss. Olivette started her own drug empire and relocated to a remote home in New Mexico, where no one would be able to find her if she didn't tell them where she was. Never again would someone control her life, and never again would she smother her emotions with medicine. If her rage came, she let it flow.

Knock! Knock!

The sound of knuckles hitting her open office door brought Olivette back to the present. The smile on her lips faded as she and her guest connected eyes. She had been expecting to see him and hoped he had news.

"Come in and sit down, Jaquies," she said and motioned to a chair on the opposite side of her desk. "I hope you have some sort of useful information on The Last Kings' operation this time. What happened to your plan? I check daily to see if Sadie Thomas is dead, and every day I am utterly let down. Before The Last Kings, do you know how much money I made in the drug business? Now I see my hard work deteriorate because of their expansion. Do you care to explain why you can't do your job efficiently?"

Jaquies—or as others called him, Jaq—entered the office and sat down. His hair was freshly braided, and he wore an expression she couldn't read on his face. He had been sent to Detroit to infiltrate Olivette's biggest competition in hopes of bringing them down from the inside a year ago. So far, he had done nothing but disappoint.

"I apologize for my impotence. I'm trying, though," Jaquies told her.

"You're trying, though?" she repeated in a dull voice.

"Yes, I'm trying. And do you know how hard it is trying to make moves without them people knowing what I'm really up to? Shit. I've been there for a year, but Sadie runs a ship as airtight as yours. I thought that by getting in the head of one of her generals and telling him how he could catch her slipping, he would kill her for us."

"But?"

"But Sadie isn't that easy to fool."

Olivette was quiet as she continued to roll the spike stick between her fingers. Jaquies appeared as if he didn't know whether to run for the door or stay frozen in his seat. Her eyes pierced through him, and she could tell by looking at the skin jumping on his neck that his heart rate had sped up. Once again, she got up from her chair, but that time she went and stood behind him. Quickly, she snatched him by his braids, pulled his head back, and pressed the spike against his exposed neck until she drew blood.

"This is the second time you've come to my home with bad news," she whispered in his ear. "You have three seconds to give me a reason why I shouldn't kill you where you sit."

"Don't . . . don't kill me," he pleaded.

"Onnnee," she said in a singsong voice.

"Please . . ."

"Twoooo." She pressed the stick tighter on his neck.

"Sadie developed a new drug," Jaquies blurted out. "She . . . she already put it on the streets."

That was exactly the kind of information Olivette was looking to hear. However, she still wasn't prepared to hear something of that magnitude. *A new drug? How?* Olivette retracted the weapon, and Jaquies took a deep, thankful breath when she went back to her seat.

"What's the name of this drug?"

"It's called *Vita E Morte*," he told her.

"Life and death," she said, recognizing the Latin words.

"Yeah. They call it VEM for short."

"And did you bring this drug with you?"

"No," he answered timidly, then sped up his speech seeing her hand grip the weapon in her hand. "But for a good reason."

"And what's the reason?"

"Because that shit turns people into zombies," he said seriously.

"Excuse me?" she said, unable to resist the laugh that came out. "Every drug does that."

"Nah, that shit is different. I've seen it for myself. The fiends in Detroit are going crazy for it. They get addicted to it faster than any other drug I've seen. It's like, once they have a taste for it, they forget about anything else they've ever liked. I pulled this up right before I got here to show you."

Jaquies reached in the pocket of his jeans and pulled out a cell phone. On it, he opened up a video that was on the internet and slid it over to her. When she picked it up, she looked on the screen and didn't see anything but a bunch of people rioting and looting stores. Some were demonstrating remarkable strength. It was pure chaos, and she didn't understand why he was showing it to her.

"What is this, Jaquies?" She slid the phone back his way. "Why are you wasting my time?"

"That's Azua, in the Dominican Republic," he told her. "From the information I've gathered, that's where Sadie and her cousin Ray began selling VEM."

"Ray?" Olivette furrowed her brows in interest. "I thought he died a while back."

"It's what they want everyone to think."

"So they have an operation there and in the States?" She was truly intrigued by the new knowledge. "Even more of a reason to end them. I want that drug, Jaquies. And I want it as soon as possible."

"But that's the thing. Nobody should have this drug," he tried to explain and shook his phone at her. The urgency in his face was what caught her attention. "You should have watched the video in its entirety and read the comments. If you did, you would understand."

"I would understand?" Olivette's eyes lowered at the audacity of him, a worker ant, telling her what she should have done.

"I didn't mean it like that," Jaquies hurried to correct himself. "I'm just saying, in the video, what you saw was people who are doing whatever they have to in order to get the drug. Some are stealing for the money. Some are killing at the dealer's command. There was a bitch who punched through glass and was unfazed by the shit. Another man who damn near lifted a car trying to rob the people in it. It's like they're controlled by the VEM and will do whatever the person who has it says to do, no matter what. Those people . . . those people aren't themselves anymore. The drug changed them."

"So, in other words, as long as Sadie is the holder of *Vita E Morte,* she contains the power to control anyone who takes it?"

"From what I can tell, yes. As long as it's still in the user's blood."

"Then that's not good for business and has just made me want it more. How did she make it?"

"I don't know."

"Where does she make it at?"

"I don't know," he said again.

"Then I suggest you find out," she said with a curled lip. "I want the formula for that drug."

And she was serious. Although she was a millionaire before she became a queenpin, the name she created for herself was the only thing she felt like she owned. Sadie didn't know how badly Olivette wanted her dead. Her days were numbered, because soon Olivette would have everything of hers. Including her new drug.

"All right." Jaq put his hands in a praying position and nodded. "You have my word. I won't come back here without something for you."

"Good," she said and watched him stand up to leave. The moment he got to the door, she said, "Shut it."

"I planned to after I left, ma'am," he assured her.

"No, I mean with you in here." She began to unbutton the top of the blazer dress she wore. "I'm horny. And why not use you as my human dildo before you leave? Shut the door. And know that if you don't make me cum, I'm going to chop one of your balls off."

Chapter 13

Back in Detroit, Rhonnie and Ahli were trying to come up with a way to tell Sadie that she needed to take VEM off the market before any more damage could be done. Ever since VEM hit the streets, there was new and unruly crime that had taken place on the news. Bodies were adding up, and no one knew the cause of the violent murders. The city had already been disorderly, but with VEM going around, things were slowly getting to be more and more out of control. It was what one could assume the crack epidemic was like, only worse. VEM was the only thing people wanted, and the supply The Last Kings had in the city was going fast. So fast that Ahli began to worry about what would happen if they ran out. They found out that it took about three days for the drug to be out of a person's system. Not to mention, it was an ugly three days. They had to bind Crazy Tina multiple times, because while she was on the drug, she was so strong and kept breaking free.

By the end of it, the house was in such bad shape. Rhonnie thought they would have to put a bullet in Crazy Tina's skull because she became a threat to their safety. Luckily, they didn't have to, but still, she could only imagine what an entire city of people going through withdrawal from VEM would look like. Unfortunately for them, Sadie hadn't returned from her trip to Azua, and it was going on a week. She also wasn't returning anyone's calls and texts, and Rhonnie could tell that her sister was getting frustrated.

They had just pulled up to the airport and were sitting outside, waiting patiently, when Rhonnie caught the foiled expression on Ahli's face. She didn't need three guesses to figure out what her sister was thinking about. Ahli hadn't really said much since they let Crazy Tina go in Petey Boy's care a few days prior.

"Everything is going to be all right," Rhonnie assured her sister from the driver's seat of her Rolls-Royce.

"How can you say that when you saw what I saw?" Ahli asked, massaging her temple. "VEM must give the user an extreme boost of adrenaline, because that bitch had super strength. I almost had to kill her."

"But you didn't, and I didn't."

"Because we didn't end up having to," Ahli reminded her. "And that was also because she was contained, but what if she weren't? Rashad called me this morning and told me how bizarre his usual folks were acting after taking a few of the pills. He said he's known some for years but almost couldn't recognize them when they came to get served again."

"A shell of themselves," Rhonnie thought aloud.

"Exactly. And what's going to happen when these fucking clucks can't afford the drug they're addicted to? What about when ten people corner one of our dealers, huh? And he or she is forced to put them motherfuckas down? Not only are those unnecessary bodies to catch, but the whole operation is going to be blazing. This shit is getting too hot too fast. It's just—"

She wasn't able to finish her sentence. Instead, she let out an angry sigh. Rhonnie had been having those same thoughts. If what had happened to Brayland happened to others, they wouldn't have a choice but to kill their customers. Everything that Angelo had told them would happen to the user of VEM was happening, and it was the scariest thing Rhonnie had ever witnessed.

"Sadie was worried about competition in the drug game coming for our throats. She didn't think for one second it would be our clients," Rhonnie said.

"Exactly. And now she's not even answering the phone." Ahli checked the gold Patek on her wrist. "I wish this nigga would hurry up. What time did his flight say it would be here, NaNa?"

"His flight landed fifteen minutes ago. He should be coming out any second. Wait! There he is."

Rhonnie pointed out the window just as Cyril was making his way out of the revolving doors with a suitcase and a duffle bag in tow. She had done like Ahli had said and reached out to him just to get some up-to-date information about the VEM he had. In short, he said that he needed to have a face-to-face with Sadie about the drug she'd given him to sell. He wouldn't give the sisters any information over the phone, so they invited him to come back to their city. What they had failed to mention was that they hadn't heard from Sadie.

Ahli rolled her window down and waved to Cyril so he would see where they were parked. He smiled and waved back before walking toward their car. Rhonnie popped the trunk and got out to help him put his things in the trunk, but he stopped her.

"I got it," he assured her in his deep, sexy voice. He had a California accent, and she liked how he pronounced his words. "You got a body in here or something?"

"Not in my baby!" Rhonnie said and rubbed a hand against the paint job of the Rolls-Royce. "She doesn't even see the battlefield too often. We have throwaway cars for all that."

"I feel it." Cyril grinned, placing his things inside the empty trunk.

The wind blew his aroma up Rhonnie's nose, and she almost did a quick, "Mmmm." He smelled marvelous. Not to mention, she didn't remember him being so tall the last time she saw him. Or good-looking for that matter. The sun shined perfectly on his smooth brown skin, and she admired his muscular build. Her eyes went to his hands, and she found herself wondering how good he was with them. She had to clear her throat to snap back to reality and stop herself from drooling. But he was fine, and she didn't know how she had overlooked him for Legacy. She got back into the front seat, and he made himself comfortable in the back.

"What's good?" he greeted Ahli, who gave him a quick nod.

"Don't mind her," Rhonnie told him. "All this VEM shit just has her tight right now."

"I bet, especially if y'all still pushing that shit in the streets."

"You're not?" Rhonnie said, glancing into the rearview mirror as she pulled away from the airport.

"Hell nah." Cyril looked out the window and didn't elaborate.

Rhonnie and Ahli shared a brief look before Rhonnie glanced back in the rearview mirror at Cyril's serious face. "I guess you're here to get your money back."

"On God, I need all my ends back. Plus compensation for the casualties."

"We can make that happen as soon as Sadie gets back in town."

"What you mean, as soon as Sadie gets back in town? She ain't here?"

"Nope."

"And you couldn't tell me that over the phone?"

"Nope. I had a feeling you wouldn't come if I told you that," Rhonnie told him.

"And you would have been right. What did you let me come for, to waste my time?"

"Because I wanted to see you," she answered boldly. "Pick your brain a little bit. Is that a problem?"

It was obvious that Cyril was caught off guard by her honesty. The hard expression he had softened ever so slightly, and he turned away from the window to meet her gaze.

"Not at all, shorty," he responded, and she saw a small smile creep to his lips. "What do you have in mind?"

"Well, we have some runs to make, so I was going to take you to the mansion while we did that. And then it's free game. How long did you plan on staying?"

"I don't know, a few days. But now that I know Sadie ain't even in town, I might skate out tonight."

"Well, before you do, I'll make sure you get all your money back."

"How you gon' do that if you're just security? Your boss ain't here to clear that kind of paper going out."

"Out of my own pocket," Rhonnie said, cutting her eyes at him. "Anything else?"

"My bad, shorty. I ain't know y'all was getting it like that."

"Yeah, well, our job is more than just being sexy in a suit."

"You do wear the fuck out of that suit. I can't even cap," Cyril said nonchalantly and started fiddling with his cell phone.

He didn't even realize that his words had placed butterflies in her stomach. She tried to hide the smile on her face, but nothing got past Ahli. She'd been sitting in the passenger's seat, witnessing Rhonnie and Cyril's little exchange. She batted her eyes at Rhonnie in a mockery, and Rhonnie fought the urge to hit her.

"He's cute!" Ahli mouthed.

"Shut up!" Rhonnie mouthed back.

"You should fuck him. Does he have a girl?"

"Y'all do know I can see you, right?"

Rhonnie's eyes jerked to the rearview, and sure enough, Cyril was staring up at them with an amused expression. She did the only thing that she could do: she burst out laughing. Ahli's face held a sheepish expression on it, and she turned to face him.

"My bad. It's just been a while since my sister liked somebody first."

"LaLa!"

"What? It has been! I'm not doing anything but telling the truth, and don't say you don't like him, because you do, and it's obvious," Ahli snapped at her before putting her attention back on Cyril. "With everything going on right now, beating around the bush just wastes time, especially if you're leaving tonight. So tell me, do you got a girl?"

"I did," Cyril answered honestly. "We had a son together."

"Well, what happened?"

"She wanted me to choose between them and the streets, and I wouldn't. Not when I just hit my prime and when I should be able to have both. She didn't trust me, and because of that, I stopped trusting her."

"So you left."

"One point for Captain Obvious." Cyril clapped silently, and that made Rhonnie laugh.

Ahli glared at both of them. Rhonnie wanted to tell her sister welcome to her world. Brayland was always making snide remarks like that, and now she knew how it felt.

"You know what? NaNa, drop me off. You two can hang out for the day."

"What about the runs?"

"I can handle them by myself." She shrugged.

"What's the run?" Cyril asked.

"We're about to go around to everyone we distributed VEM to and take back their supply," Rhonnie said before shooting Ahli a look. "And these niggas aren't going to like you coming into their spot, demanding their product back."

"I said I'll be fine," Ahli tried to assure her again.

"I hate to say it, but little sis is right. You are the little sister, right?" Cyril asked, looking at Rhonnie, who smiled with a nod.

"See?" she shot at Ahli. "You don't need to go alone."

"And what would you know about it?" Ahli asked Cyril, turning her nose up at him. "You haven't seen what I can do."

"I don't need to see what you can do to tell you that a large group of men won't take it well when a woman is coming into their spot, telling them what to do. Especially if the VEM is making them a lot of money."

"So I'm going with you! We can drop Cyril off at the mansion and handle the business."

"Nah, I'm coming."

"We can't risk your safety while you're in town," Ahli told him. "While you're here, especially under our personal invite, our jobs are to keep you safe."

"I'm coming," Cyril said, disregarding everything she had said. "Also, I don't let just anybody guard me. I'm curious to see why Sadie chose y'all to be her special security detail. Plus, after all, I'm part of The Last Kings now. Your business is my business. All I need is a gun."

There was silence in the car as they rode on the highway before Ahli finally nodded and spoke.

"All right. Let's do it."

Their first stop was to Rashad, and it wasn't hard to get him to return all the VEM he had in his possession. He was glad to get rid of it, noting to tell Sadie that he would just stick with his regular order from then on. In fact, the first few stops were like that. All of them were happy to get rid of the drug, and Rhonnie felt that they must have had some sort of run-in with the second stage of it. By the time they reached Gerron, their last stop, they were confident that things would go smoothly.

Gerron was an up-and-coming music producer, and he opened his studio, G Waves, with the money he made from trapping. After working with a few heavy hitters in the rap game, he had been getting some major buzz. He'd been rocking with The Last Kings for about three years. For a while, Sadie laundered money through the music studio and just gave Gerron a bigger piece of the pie. However, when someone was shot and murdered in the parking lot of G Waves, she pulled the plug on that. Gerron had Feds sniffing around his place of business and looking closely at his books. Sadie didn't want to take any chances. Luckily, nothing was found, but Sadie hadn't cleaned her money with his studio since.

Rhonnie parked the Rolls-Royce in the handicap spot in the parking lot of the studio, closest to the entrance, and they got out. The air around the building smelled loudly of Kush, and the bouncer standing outside the door mugged the sisters as if he had never seen them a day in his life. His eyes lingered on Cyril as they approached, and before they could enter the building, he held an arm out.

"What's your business here?" his deep voice sounded.

"Damn, Shane, we can't go up in the studio?" Rhonnie feigned like she was insulted.

"You ain't no recording artist, and the boss wasn't expecting you," Shane told her and then nodded toward Cyril. "And who is this nigga? Gerron doesn't like it when nonpaying customers pop up."

"Well, lucky for you, Debo, I ain't a customer," Cyril told him in a bored voice.

"I don't know you, so I can't let you enter," Shane said, stepping forward with his chest out.

The two of them were around the same height, but Shane was more muscular. Which didn't seem to faze Cyril at all. He stood his ground and stared back into Shane's growling face with an unimpressed expression.

"Do you know who they are?" Cyril asked, nodding at the women with him.

"Yes."

"What's their names?"

"Rhonnie and Ahli."

"And who do they represent?"

"Nigga, this ain't no fuckin' test. I don't gotta—" Before Shane could finish his sentence, Cyril had the Glock he'd been given pointed at his nose.

"I believe I said, who do they represent, nigga?"

"Sadie," Shane answered quickly.

"And do you know who I am?"

"I just said I ain't never seen you before."

"Well, let me introduce myself. I'm Cyril Anderson," Cyril told him, and the scowl Shane wore disappeared.

"I know that name. Aren't you Cane Anderson's brother?"

"The one and the only."

Not only did Shane stand down, but there was an expression of respect that came over his face. It was a look that Rhonnie had only seen people around there give Sadie when she decided to show her face. Rhonnie was fascinated, to say the least. There she was, thinking Cyril was just a young boss. She had forgotten that quickly that he was a kingpin.

"M . . . my bad, boss. Don't kill me. I heard rumors that you were down with Sadie, but I didn't know how true they were. Not with you holding shit down in Cali."

"What do you know about what I do in Cali?"

"Shit, you a savage. You have a lot of respect in a lot of places. They say you're even more of a menace than your brother was."

"Yeah, losing the person you love more than yourself does that to you," Cyril told him and lowered his gun.

"Here, let me get that for you," Shane told them and held the door open. "He's in recording room C."

When they walked into the building, it was apparent where the strong smell of Kush was coming from. The hallways were dark, and the only lighting came from the red bulbs in the light fixtures on the ceiling. The walls were filled with frames that held the top records of Gerron's artists.

"Dog has a nice spot here," Cyril commended him.

"I just hope it's still as nice by the time we leave," Ahli said. "Gerron has a mean streak. And he hates people dropping by unannounced."

"Mean streak or not, there should be some common sense in his head. VEM is bad for business, and ain't no point in keeping something that's not going to be on the market anymore."

"Sadie's not gon' sell it anymore?" Cyril asked.

"Well, we haven't gotten that far yet," Rhonnie said as quickly and softly as she could, but he still heard her.

"Wait," he said and stopped in his tracks. "She don't know y'all out here snatching the VEM back?"

"Well . . ." Rhonnie tried to think of a nice way to put it, but she couldn't come up with anything. "No. No, she doesn't."

"And y'all don't think she's gon' be pissed when she finds out y'all are out here moving on your own accord?"

"She probably is."

"And you don't care?"

"Sometimes you have to go against something you love for the greater good."

"And I can't go another day with that shit being out there," Ahli rang in. "Sadie is just gon' have to do what she does when she finds out. But when she sees what that shit does to people, what it's doing to the city, she'll understand."

"And you're sure? Sadie seems like someone all about her money."

"Don't let that cold exterior fool you," Ahli warned. "She has a heart somewhere in that chest of hers. If you stick around long enough, you might be lucky to see it one day."

"Yeah, a'ight," Cyril said, looking at them as if they were crazy. "Let's just go get this shit and bounce. I need to shower."

They walked until they found recording room C in the back of the studio and didn't bother to knock before entering. Sitting in a comfortable-looking chair in front of the digital audio workstation was Gerron, but he wasn't alone. His head was thrown back in pure bliss as two of the thickest naked women Rhonnie had ever seen took turns pleasuring him. One of them had a chocolate complexion, and the other was fair-skinned. Gerron had literally been caught lacking with his pants down.

"Shane, get the fuck out of here until I'm done with these whores," Gerron said, not caring to look and see who had entered. "Can't you see I'm getting my dick wet?"

"We sure do," Ahli spoke up and leaned against one of the walls with her arms crossed. "I thought that thing would be bigger than that. But then again, you can't always judge a man's size by his *size*."

Gerron whipped his head around, and when he saw the three of them, he shoved the women's heads away from him and pulled his jeans up. In that moment, his light skin was a dead giveaway for his feathers being ruffled. His cheeks had turned a bright, rosy red, and he glared at them as he tucked his gun back into his waist. The women didn't seem to be ashamed. Instead, they just stood up and held their hands out.

"I ain't giving you whores shit. Weak-ass head. Get the fuck out of here," he said and waved his arm forcefully to the door before fixing the collar on his Versace shirt.

"Hell nah, Gerron!" the chocolate woman exclaimed. "You not shorting me again, nigga. You ain't fuckin' broke! I want my money."

"Yeah, nigga. You always tryin'a get a nut off but not pay a bitch. Run us our paper."

"Is this what you do with your free time and money?" Rhonnie asked, taking a seat on a stool with wheels. She reached into the inside pocket of her suit and pulled out a small roll of money before throwing it at the women. "That's two bands. Split it. I can't see y'all charging more than that for that wack-ass head."

"Now get the fuck out of here. We have shit to do," Ahli chimed in.

The women seemed happy and scooped their clothes up from the corner of the room. When they were gone, Gerron eyed his new visitors angrily, but curiously. "What did I do to have the honor of having Sadie's mutts show up at my place of business?"

"I'll choose to ignore that," Rhonnie told him. "We're here on business."

"What kind of business? I wasn't expecting you."

"VEM business," Ahli said.

"What about it? The shit's a gold mine. I've re-upped twice already. Waiting for one of my young niggas to come grab the pack now," Gerron said, shrugging his shoulders as if he were trying to figure out the problem.

"Well, we need it back," Rhonnie told him.

"You need it back?" Gerron looked at her as if she were speaking another language. When he saw that she was serious, he gave a deep belly laugh.

"Yeah. Now."

"I already bought it, it's mine, and I ain't giving it back," Gerron told her. "This is the kind of business Sadie conducts? Sell a product and send her henchmen to rob a nigga?"

"You can get back whatever you spent on it. We just need that pack."

"Nah, 'cause what I spent on it ain't nearly as much as they bring home when I flip it. So that's a no-go." Gerron shrugged again. "I guess your business here has concluded. You found your way in, so I assume you know your way out."

"You ignorant motherfucka, have you seen what that shit is doing to people?" Ahli asked and stood up straight.

"You mean all that crazy shit on the news? Hell yeah," Gerron chuckled. "I actually got some fiends handling some business in Flint for me right now thinking they're gon' get a free pop of VEM. That's good business for both of us. No blood on my hands, and they get to get high. It's a win-win."

"Are you stupid?" Rhonnie made a face.

"No, the question is, are *you* stupid? Shit, I had a CEO for some internet farming company scratching at the studio door a few days ago before I re-upped on them pills. Said he would give me every dollar in his bank account if I gave him a hundred of those bad boys. I could see it in his eyes that he *needed* the VEM. These motherfuckas are turning into fiends overnight!"

"And you don't see a problem with that?" Rhonnie asked, dumbfounded.

"I don't give a fuck, as long as they're paying *me.* I've never seen anything like it."

"You're sick."

"We're all in the game for one thing: the money. Would you be Sadie's mutt if she didn't pay you?" he asked, and when she was quiet, he gave her a knowing look. "I didn't think so. Shit, I'ma have to find out what's in them pills and go into business for myself, but I doubt Sadie will share. But I can handle that."

"You gon' say that so boldly in front of us?" Ahli asked with a twitching hand.

"Another thing I don't give a fuck about is the feelings of a mutt. When I run things, maybe you can come work for me. I'll even pay extra if you throw that ass back."

"No," Ahli warned Rhonnie when she went to make a move on Gerron for the disrespect.

"Yeah, listen to big sis, mutt," Gerron chuckled. "Fuck Sadie. Do you know how much it affected my business when she made the choice to not pay me to wash her money anymore?"

"That sounds like a personal problem. You weren't washing the money anymore, so why would she still pay you?"

"She didn't pay me for the last month I did, and she should have. She said that it was my punishment for not running a tight-enough ship. I was gon' open up another studio with that money, but I lost the bid on the building because she ain't give me what she owed."

"I wouldn't have paid you either," Ahli told him. "You were too hot, and that's bad for business. Had the Feds sniffing all in and around this motherfucka. She let you keep your life. That's payment enough. You're lucky that she's even still breaking bread with you."

"Barely. She still got me on a probational period like I'm a fucking child. If it weren't for VEM being new, I'm sure she wouldn't have let me try it out or re-up."

"You niggas are always switching up for some petty shit," Rhonnie spat, shaking her head.

"It's real enough to me," Gerron countered.

"Yeah, whatever. Listen, we're not here to listen to you vent about some crybaby shit. We're here for the VEM, and we're not leaving without it."

"That's not up for debate," Cyril's voice finally sounded. "Give us the pack so we can be on our way."

Gerron blinked at him. It was as if he were noticing Cyril for the first time. After a brief stare-down, Gerron began laughing hysterically. "And who the fuck are you?"

"The kingpin of L.A. Cyril Anderson, nigga."

"Oh." Gerron stopped laughing immediately to look Cyril up and down. When his eyes stopped on Cyril's face, he nodded. "Come to think of it, you do look just like that nigga Cane, just darker. I met him back in the day, you know. Back when I was just a runner. That was a solid motherfucka right there. I didn't think anybody could put him down, but just like any dog with rabies, it happened."

Cyril became a blur. That was how fast he moved. Before Rhonnie even had time to take another breath, he had Gerron in a chokehold. Gerron tried to reach for his gun, but Rhonnie already had hers aimed at him.

"If he was a dog with rabies, then I guess I am too. And if you don't tell us where the VEM is, you're about to find out what happens when you get bit by one," Cyril snarled and placed the barrel of his gun on Gerron's temple.

"Do I need to remind you that you're in my place of business?" Gerron choked out slowly as his airway was being constricted.

He was close to his equipment bar, and Rhonnie failed to see him press one of the buttons. The next thing they all knew, three men toting AR rifles came in and blocked the recording room door. They aimed their weapons at the three unwelcomed guests while Rhonnie and Ahli aimed their own guns at them. They were outnumbered, and Rhonnie knew if those rifles got to barking, there wouldn't be much left of them to clean up in that closed-in room. Gerron smirked, seeing that his cavalry had arrived.

"I'm not giving you shit. Let me go, or they die," he warned Cyril victoriously.

"See, one thing about soldiers is, if they're loyal, they're taught to defend their boss at all costs," Cyril said into Gerron's ear while looking at the three men. "And they will. If his life is in danger, they know not to make a move until he's safe. They'll even risk their own lives to get him to safety. And if he dies, they'll avenge his death no matter what. However, that's *only* if they're loyal. On the other hand, they could be disloyal. If their boss is dead, there isn't anyone to pay them. So, why get revenge when they have to spend their time finding a new connect? I'm interested to see how this will play out."

"What are you waiting for, you fucking idiots!" Gerron said to his men. "Kill them n—"

Boom!

The shot from Cyril's gun rang loudly. The bullet struck Gerron in one temple and took a chunk of his head when it went out the other, silencing him permanently. Cyril released his body and let it drop to the floor. The men toting the automatic weapons were dazed and confused at the turn of events. They didn't know what to do, and in their moment of confusion, they lowered their weapons, which proved to be a regrettable decision. Rhonnie and Ahli didn't hesitate to fill their bodies up with their bullets. The men's bodies jerked ferociously, and right as they were falling to the ground, Shane appeared in the doorway. He saw Gerron dead on the ground, as well as the young soldiers, and went for his own weapon.

"Ah ah, I would tread very lightly if I were you," Cyril said, aiming his gun at Shane's face again. "Tell us where your boss stashed his packs, and there might be something in it for you."

Shane glanced at Gerron's dead body again as if he were contemplating his next move. Rhonnie took a few steps and kicked Gerron in the side, proving to Shane that he was dead.

"Your boss is dead, which means he's never coming back. So that gives you a few choices. You can either join them on the ground with a bullet in your head, or you can accept this offer."

"What's the offer?" he asked.

"If Gerron is gone, then that means this place needs a new owner," she told him. "I'm even willing to give you the money he spent on the VEM he purchased. But first, you have to show us where it is. Next, we need you to dump these bodies somewhere that nobody will ever find them."

"You can make sure G Waves belongs to me?"

"Yes."

"And I can rename it S Waves?"

"I would come up with something a little more original than that, but yeah, sure. Whatever you want. Now, will you show us to the drugs?"

Shane nodded and waved for them to follow him. "It's this way."

Chapter 14

Jaq left New Mexico almost as quickly as he had landed. There wasn't a person on the earth who put more fear in his heart than Olivette. The woman had to be the spawn of Satan. He had been worried that his dick wouldn't be able to get hard for her, but when she stripped and he saw her naked body, his manhood rose to the occasion. She'd made him feel like a human blow-up doll and used him for her own sick pleasure. He had felt helpless as she rode him like a horse in her office chair, and he was just happy to be back in Detroit, where he didn't feel like a little bitch. However, he still was Olivette's bitch, no matter where he was. Now his only objective was getting the formula of VEM for her.

The second he was home that night, he put his plan into motion. Knowing that the men he had working under him were loyal to Sadie first, Olivette had assembled a team for Jaq to bring back with him. They, like Jaq, would do whatever it took to keep her happy. Anything to keep them as far away from her wrath as possible.

The first step was getting all the VEM The Last Kings had in the city. He knew there was only one place Sadie would keep it. She had many stash spots across town and even some in Flint, but he knew there was only one place that she would keep the VEM: her grandmother's house. Jaq had only been through there once or twice with Brayland. In fact, Brayland was the one who told him that it used to be her grandmother's house. It was in a neighborhood that was heavily guarded and a place no one dared to disrespect. Most of the houses were smaller and belonged to the elderly. It was a place where no one would ever expect anything bad to happen, which was how he knew that was where she would keep the VEM and its formula.

Jaq and the men pulled up at the end of the block in the neighborhood inside of a white van and prepared for battle. It was one of Sadie's vehicles, one that anyone working under her would recognize and not question. Since it was dark outside, they wore tactical night goggles over their face masks. Jaq made sure the muzzle was on his gun and armed himself with extra clips.

"Team one, it might be quiet, but there is a man at every house," he instructed the men in the van and pointed at the houses in front of them. "Right there, there, there, and there. I need you to clear them out for team two to make it to the house. Radio back when the job is done.

Team two, once you're inside of the house, I want you to make sure nobody is left alive. Team three, I'm with you. We'll load up all of the VEM they have inside. We have to move fast. The Last Kings aren't like any other operation I've ever seen. Each person manning a stash spot is required to check in every hour on the nose. And when the soldier manning this spot doesn't check in when he's supposed to, I want to be long gone by the time they send someone to check it out. I also want clean kills. I don't want anyone to be tipped off to what's going on here. Understand?"

"Yes, sir!" they all said in unison.

"Team one, move out," Jaq said and made a gesture with his hand.

Three of the men in the truck exited without a second instruction to do so. Jaq sat confidently as he watched them maneuver down the sidewalks. Crouched down low, they became one with the shadows of the cars parked on the street. Their feet moved silently, like a lion sneaking up on its prey. They were the best at what they did. That was why Olivette had sent them. He observed them in the distance swiftly take out each one of the men he had pointed out in their hiding spots.

"Team two, you're clear," a man's voice said through the radio in Jaq's lap.

"You heard him, go! Remember, no survivors," Jaq directed, and three more men got out.

That time, the wait was a little longer. Jaq felt his anxiety hit its peak and prepared to drive out of there fast if something had gone wrong. Just as he was fearing the worst, he heard the radio crackle.

"They're all down, sir. Team three is clear."

Jaq drove the van up to the house and backed into the driveway. He and the remaining two passengers hopped out and made their way into the home. The house was still fully furnished as if an elderly lady lived there. There were even dishes in the kitchen sink. But that didn't fool Jaq. He headed straight for the stairs while the others scoured the first level of the house.

It was obvious that the small home had been renovated, with its up-to-date appliances and newer hardwood flooring. In the basement, there was a skinny hallway that led to a door. Jaq stepped over the dead bodies of Sadie's soldiers until he got to the slightly ajar door. Sure enough, there in front of him on one table was a large amount of money, and on the other was a big duffle bag of pills.

Jaq was confused, though. From the looks of it, the men hadn't been in the middle of packaging them. He could tell by the wrinkled used Baggies on the floor around the tables. It looked as if they had been pouring the Baggies into one big bag. He didn't give it too much thought, though. He ransacked the basement in search of something that said what was in the drug, but he didn't find anything. Not even a single piece of paper. Not wanting to waste any more time, he gave up on that search. He ignored the money and just grabbed the bag of pills that felt heavy on his shoulder before leaving the same way he'd entered.

"I got it!" he said in a hurry when he materialized from the basement.

"There's nothing up here, sir," one of the men told him. "It's clean as a whistle."

"One out of two is still a win," Jaq said. "Let's go."

"What about the house, sir?" the same man asked as they filed out into the van.

"Burn it to the ground," Jaq said. He handed the man matches and another can of gasoline that were in the back of the vehicle. "And do it quickly. We have one more stop to make."

Chapter 15

Rhonnie paced back and forth in her suite, trying to decide what she was going to do. They'd been back at the mansion for some hours after dropping at a stash spot all the VEM that hadn't been distributed out to the city. Of course, some had sold pills to customers, but as fast as the clients were coming back, Rhonnie knew the VEM still on the streets would be gone quickly. Ahli had tried again to contact Sadie when they got home, but it went straight to voicemail. She would just have to find out the news when she got back. The thought of her trying to kill them was the least of Rhonnie's worries at the moment. Right then, she was trying to get up the courage to go down to the guest room quarters and knock on Cyril's door. She'd just gotten out of the shower and changed from a suit into a casual pair of skinny jeans, an off-the-shoulder sweatshirt, and her favorite pair of Chanel slippers.

"He's just a man," Rhonnie coached herself. "You've killed a few of those before, so why are you so nervous?"

And she was absolutely and positively the most nervous she'd ever been. He had tagged along with them to see how they operated, when in turn, they actually got to see how he moved. The way he handled business at Gerron's was the sexiest thing she'd witnessed in a long time. He didn't even flinch when he saw the assault rifles pointed their way. Gone was the confident woman she normally was. She'd been replaced by a timid girl she'd never met before. Rhonnie was intimidated, to say the least, and not only that, but Gerron's words had gotten to her. What would Cyril find interesting about a mutt? She wasn't a boss like him and Sadie. They worked for themselves. She worked for them.

"Nope, I'm not doing it." Rhonnie threw her hands up in frustration. "But what did I call him here for if I'm not going to at least talk to him?"

She continued to go back and forth with herself before finally deciding she was going to leave it alone. It would be unprofessional to hit on one of Sadie's business partners, especially while he was a guest in her home. Slightly let down, Rhonnie decided a carton of Ben & Jerry's would cheer her up. She grabbed her cell phone and left the room. When she opened her bedroom door, she had to lean back quickly to avoid getting hit in the face by a huge fist.

"My bad, shorty. I didn't know the door was gon' open when I went to knock on it."

There Cyril was standing with a smile on his face. He too had showered and was dressed casually in a Balenciaga T-shirt, Amiri jeans, and a pair of all-white G-Fazos. Rhonnie was so shocked that her lips moved, but no words came out. That made Cyril's smile turn into a laugh.

"You good?" he asked. "I could have sworn my fist ain't connect with your head, but I could be wrong."

"No. I mean, yes, I'm good!" Rhonnie blurted. "You just caught me off guard, that's all."

"Is it a bad time? I could come back later."

"No, it's fine. Did you need something?"

"I was actually tryin'a find my way to the kitchen, but this damn house is so big, I got lost on the way. Ahli told me you would show me how to get there."

"I'm sure she did," Rhonnie responded, knowing that Ahli thought she was slick. "I was on my way down there myself to get some ice cream. Come on, you can follow me."

She shut the door behind her and led Cyril to the stairwell that would take them to the first level of the house. She had to admit, it would be easy for someone to get lost in the mansion if they didn't know their way around. But common sense would be that the kitchen was on the lower level of the home. Had he just wanted an excuse to come talk to her?

Stop being ridiculous, Rhonnie.

"Ice cream, huh?" Cyril asked as they journeyed down the stairs. "You must have something on your mind."

"Why do you say that?"

"Because it's late afternoon, and correct me if I'm wrong, but I don't think you've eaten since we got back."

"How would you know? You've been in your room for the past two hours."

"Is it normal for y'all to clock your guests' every move while they're here?"

"Is it regular where you're from for the guest to clock the stomach of the host? This way."

They stepped off the staircase, and he continued to follow her all the way to the large kitchen. He sat on one of the stools at the island, and Rhonnie headed right to the freezer. From it, she grabbed a small carton of her favorite flavor and shook it at Cyril to see if he wanted one.

"It's either this or frozen pizza," she told him. "Nobody cooks much around here anymore. We're always on the go."

"I get it. I'll take the ice cream."

She tossed him a carton and grabbed another for herself before letting the door shut. After getting them both spoons, she leaned against the island across from him and opened her carton. Rhonnie paused briefly, noticing something different about the kitchen. She looked around and saw that Sadie must have replaced many of the appliances that were on the counters. It was strange, because Rhonnie didn't remember the last time she'd seen Sadie use the ones they had before. They were practically brand new. She shrugged it off, thinking that maybe Sadie just wanted to change things up a bit.

"You never told me what's on your mind." Cyril's voice interrupted her thoughts.

"I don't think I ever said there was anything on it."

"You don't have to. It's all over your face."

Rhonnie shrugged her shoulders and took a big bite of her ice cream. It was creamy and delightful, just like she knew it would be. But it didn't calm the butterflies flying madly in her stomach. Being that close to a man never had that kind of effect on her. But just hearing his voice and smelling his scent was doing something to her that she couldn't explain. She found herself wondering if his lips would be soft on hers and if his hands would be rough against her back. But she couldn't tell him that.

"Well, if you won't say anything, how about I ask you some questions?"

"Shoot." Rhonnie shrugged.

"How long have you and your sister been working for The Last Kings?"

"About three years," Rhonnie answered.

"How did all that come about? I mean, how did y'all work your way up in the ranks to the position you have now?"

"We didn't. We got the jobs the moment we agreed to be part of this operation."

"Damn," Cyril said, openly impressed. "Y'all must really be something then."

"Yeah, maybe. She saved us, and for that, we are indebted to her."

"Is that the only reason you do your job?" Cyril asked and stared at her curiously.

"At first, yeah," she answered honestly. "But now it's different."

"Different how?"

"I love her," Rhonnie said simply, and that time Cyril raised his eyebrow. "Not in that way, stupid."

"So, you love her because she pays you well?"

"She does, but that's not it." She shook her head with a small smile. "The Sadie the world sees is different from the Sadie my sister and I see. She's one of the most amazing people I've ever met in my life. She's not this cold-hearted bitch who stands over us with a whip like everybody assumes. She's a mentor and a friend. And we're not just mutts to her."

She averted her eyes on her last sentence, but she felt his burning a hole in her face. For a while, nobody said a word. The nervous jitters had taken control over her again, and she was scared to look up.

"That's kind of how it was with my big brother. He was my best friend and mentor," Cyril said finally. "Back before I was who I am now, I used to bang with him and the other Bankroll Crips."

"Bankroll Crips?" Rhonnie tried, but she couldn't hide her smirk when she peeked back up at him.

"Hey, no disrespect will be tolerated," he said with a smile. "Yeah, we were called Bankroll because we stayed all about our paper. Cane, my brother, was the leader. And when he died, the crew became my responsibility."

"What happened to him, if you don't mind me asking?"

"Nah, you're good. He got caught lacking by the pussy-ass kingpin at the time. My brother put in some work for him, and in the end, the kingpin bit him like the snake he was."

"Damn, I'm sorry."

"Sorry ain't gon' bring my brother back," Cyril said somberly. "Even though I wish it would. At the time, I wished I could go back and change some shit, but I couldn't. So I handled shit in another way, the street way."

"You killed the kingpin."

"And took his job," Cyril added. "I do it better, too."

"I'm sure you do." Rhonnie tried to give him a smile, but it didn't change the look on his face. "If you could, would you?"

"Would I what?"

"Go back and change things? Bring your brother back? Go back to gang banging and getting money with the other Crips?"

Cyril pondered the question and didn't say anything at first. He just went back to eating from the carton in his hand until the ice cream was all gone. She had only asked because if someone gave her the choice to bring her dad, Quinton, back, she would do it in a heartbeat. Rhonnie was about to say something else to change the subject when Cyril finally answered.

"No," he said simply.

"No? But I thought you missed him." Rhonnie was confused.

"I do, sometimes so much that it hurts." Cyril dropped his empty carton on the counter. "The old me would have said yes to that question faster than a heartbeat. But now? I know that everything that happened happened for a reason. I might not like it or know the complete reason, but who am I to question the universe? I'm just a small dot in its design. I also know that my brother might not be here in the flesh, but he's here." Cyril touched his chest and then his temple. "Cane will always be with me. The lessons he taught me didn't leave just because he died. And if I fold just because I'm sad, then what use were those lessons at all? He taught me how to be a man, and every day I just try to add to that. He would be proud of me. I know it."

"I know he would too," Rhonnie told him. "I hope my father would be proud of me. He taught Ahli and me everything we know."

"You mean these skills I have yet to see?"

"Boy, you better stop playing with me." Rhonnie raised her eyebrow and jerked her neck slightly. "You saw how we laid them niggas down back there."

"Touché," Cyril said, unable to resist the laughter that expelled from his mouth. "Y'all did handle business back there. And you didn't flinch either. I like that."

"You do?" Rhonnie felt her face growing hot.

"Yeah, I do. Tell me about your dad."

"He was a good man, a cautious man. He taught us how to fight in combat and how to shoot. Before Ahli and I worked for Sadie, we lived in Nebraska and were professional thieves," she started. "We had to get money, and we did what we had to. We lived a good life, a rich life off the riches of others. One of the biggest licks we hit was when we robbed The Last Kings."

"So, that dude Arrik at the meeting?" Cyril asked, and Rhonnie could see the light bulb turn on over his head.

"Yeah, we robbed that nigga. But back then, he wasn't family." Rhonnie laughed, but it faded quickly. "My dad was killed soon after that. All our lives, we didn't know it, but we had a target on our backs. We thought that he had taught us these skills to rob people, but really it was to defend ourselves when the inevitable came knocking at our door."

"What do you mean?"

"Our mother was a forced escort for this scary-ass bitch named Madame," Rhonnie said and felt chills come over her when she spoke the woman's name. "My dad saved her way back in the day, and they started a family. But she took something with her when they left. Something that Madame wanted desperately."

"What?"

"The formula to *Vita E Morte*. My mother hid it away before she died, but Madame never stopped looking for it. And when she finally caught up to us, she killed my father. We found him in a pool of his own blood."

Rhonnie had to stop talking for a moment. That image of her father was one that she had always tried to keep at bay. It was the day her heart shattered into tiny pieces. She took a shaky breath and steadied herself so that she wouldn't cry in front of Cyril. When she was sure that she could go on, she cleared her throat and started talking again.

"By a sick coincidence, Ahli and I ended up in Madame's brothel, and she almost killed us in search of the formula, but then Sadie turned up and killed her first. At the time, we were just thieves to her, and she was trying to get back what belonged to her, but she ended up saving us. She gave us a new home and a new purpose. We needed her and . . . and I think she needed us too."

"A perfect design," Cyril said in awe at her story.

"Huh?"

"Everything happens for a reason. Sometimes death births new life. If Cane hadn't died, I wouldn't be the person I am today. And if your father hadn't died, then you wouldn't be here."

"If none of that had happened, VEM wouldn't be on the streets," Rhonnie sighed and shook her head. "I should have paid attention to Ahli."

"There's no way you could have known that this was gon' happen though, Rhonnie," he reasoned. "It's not your fault. All that matters now is that you're making good on the bad. Plus . . ."

"Plus what?"

"I wouldn't be here talking to you if this shit weren't happening." The look he gave her was suggestive, and he reached across the island to grab her hand. "After all this shit is over, and the streets aren't filled with drugged-up fiends, maybe we can go out sometime?"

"That depends."

"On what?"

"On your situation."

"What about my situation?" he asked.

"With your son's mom. Y'all still be fucking?"

"What kind of question is that?" He laughed at her serious expression.

"A good one," Rhonnie said and took a deep breath. She figured it was a good time to be honest with him about the things she was feeling. "The last dude

I was with played me, and I don't even want to go on a date with a nigga who has shit going on in the background. I'm not even going to front on you, Cyril. You give me butterflies I've never felt before. And that scares me. I've committed more crimes than I can count, but none of them made me as nervous as I am right now, sitting across from you."

"I make you nervous?"

"Yes. You intimidate me. Because I'm just the security, and you're a boss. So if your only agenda is to fuck me, just say that."

"Well, one, when I look at you, I don't just see you as security. I see a beautiful woman, one of the most beautiful I've seen in a while. And two, if my only agenda were to fuck you, you would be buck-naked on this island, taking my dick right now," he told her, looking deeply into her eyes.

Why did he have to say that? Rhonnie felt a rushing river begin to flow between her legs, and she inhaled briskly. So he was a freak. She was really interested now.

"But as you can see, you're still standing there completely clothed, and my dick is still in my pants. To answer your other question, nah. I'm not still fucking the mother of my son. There was a time when I loved her deeply, but sometimes things end. She picked her side, and I picked mine. And that's just that on that. As far as any other women, I dabble sometimes."

"Explain dabble."

"I have needs, the same ones I'm sure you have. If I want to fuck, I do. But have I caught feelings for the females throwing pussy my way? No."

"Why not?"

"They're like rats: all they want is your cheese. Plus, I haven't met one who can handle my lifestyle. Any other questions, shorty? You still ain't asked my favorite color."

"What's your favorite color then, smart-ass?" Rhonnie asked, embarrassed.

"Any color you're wearing," he said, making her smile. "Now, answer my question. Can I take you out sometime?"

"Yes."

They held each other's gaze, completely smitten with each other, until Rhonnie struck up the nerve to make a move. Nothing in her life had ever gone by the books, and she was a grown woman. If she wanted to kiss a man she basically had just met, so be it. She rounded the island, and he turned sideways on the stool to meet her. She didn't stop walking until she was so close to him that her breasts almost touched his face. She felt his hands slide around her waist and grip the small of her back. He raised his head, and she could smell a mixture of minty freshness and chocolate on his breath. Slowly, she lowered her face to his, and his eyes froze on her lips in anticipation.

Right when their mouths were about to meet, they heard a throat clear. Their heads jerked to the kitchen entrance, and Rhonnie jumped away from Cyril when she saw Sadie standing there. She looked like she had had a rough week. Her hair was pulled back, and she wasn't in her normal business attire. Instead, she wore a pair of jeans and a black hoodie. She took the hood off her head and furrowed her brows at both Cyril and Rhonnie.

"I would ask what the hell has been going on in my absence, but we have bigger things to discuss. Where's Ahli?"

Chapter 16

"I'm taking VEM off the market." Sadie's voice was bitter and stern.

She, Ahli, Rhonnie, Tyler, and, for some reason, Cyril were all in one of the sitting areas of the mansion. Sadie was taken aback by the surprised reactions from both Rhonnie and Ahli. She waited for them to say something, but instead, they sat there with shocked expressions. She thought for sure they would be pleased with the new revelation, especially Ahli. Or at least ask what had brought it on.

"Did you hear what I just said?" she asked, and they nodded.

"Why?" Ahli asked and then put her hands up in a "whoa" fashion. "I mean, I'm happy. But what made you change your mind? I thought money was the motive."

"I guess not all money is good money," Sadie said and looked at Tyler.

"Tell them," he urged.

"Tell us what?" Rhonnie asked.

She leaned forward from where she sat on the couch next to her sister and gave Sadie a strange look. Sadie sighed. She had hoped that she would be able to just take the drug off the market without the explanation—the freakish and inexplicable explanation of why there was no way that she would allow VEM to swarm the streets any more than it already had.

"Ray called us to come to Azua. That's where I've been this whole time when you were calling me."

"And you weren't answering," Rhonnie annoyingly threw in and pursed her lips when she caught the look Sadie gave her.

"As I said," Sadie continued, "Tyler and I went to Azua, and I thought he just wanted me to observe firsthand the effects VEM had on the patients in the lab. But . . . but I had no idea. You couldn't have paid me to expect the kind of mayhem I walked into. . . ."

The moment Sadie stepped off the private plane and saw Ray leaning on his Bentley truck, she knew something was wrong. He was wearing a fitted suit, and she was happy to see that the hair restoration surgery he'd undergone a few years back had the hair on top of his head flourishing. She wanted him to grow his locs back, but he said that stage of his life was over. He was happy with a low fade and crisp line up. Even with him looking like a million bucks, she could tell just by looking at his face that something was off. She didn't remember the last time she'd seen her cousin look so worried.

"We jumped the gun on this, Say," Ray said as soon as she got to the truck.

"What do you mean?" she asked.

"I'll show you."

She and Tyler loaded their luggage and got inside of the vehicle. Sadie thought that first she would be going to visit Adrianna, Ray's fiancée and a longtime member of The Last Kings, since it had been so long since she'd seen her. But Ray didn't take them to his home. Instead, he drove them to the lab. The outside of the building was still very much intact, but when they went inside, that was a different story.

It looked as if a few wild animals had been let free inside of it. Light fixtures hung loosely from the ceiling, glass was broken on the ground, materials were strewn everywhere, and the electrical wiring had been pulled from the wall in some places. Sadie's eyes fell on the bloody handprints smeared on the walls everywhere she looked.

"Damn!" Tyler exclaimed, looking around. "What the hell?"

"What happened here?" Sadie turned wide-eyed to Ray, who shook his head.

"Like I said, we jumped the gun."

"I . . . I don't get it."

"The VEM, Say," he told her. "It changed the patients. I don't know how or why, but it did. Come look at the footage our security cameras caught."

They followed him to where the security console was, and he flipped on the screen. He had to do some rewinding, but when he pressed play, Sadie was left with her mouth open. She had faced the evils of the men who thirsted for power, but she had never seen anything like what she was witnessing on that small screen.

The video had no sound, but Sadie watched in horror as a scientist hurried to lock the door of a female patient who was no more than 120 pounds. The patient picked up the desk in her room and flung it at the large window separating her from the scientist. When the window crashed open, the scientist tried to run, but the patient picked up a glass shard and violently slit his throat. But she didn't stop there. When he was on the ground, bleeding out, the woman jumped on him and stabbed him six more times before digging in his pocket. From it, she pulled out a small bag of pills, one of which she popped immediately. Ray turned the screen off shortly after that.

"At first, the patients were happy," Ray explained. "In fact, they were enjoying the best highs of their lives. But then they just shut off. All they wanted was their next fix. They didn't talk about what the drug made them feel. They only expressed that they needed more . . . and more. When my scientists tried to withhold the drug until they answered their questions, they attacked and killed more than half of my staff."

As he spoke, Sadie knew it was true, because she'd seen it for herself.

"Did she just pick up that desk and throw it through that window?" she asked.

"Yes," Ray confirmed and looked at them both seriously. "It would have taken two men to lift it, but she did it effortlessly. They were all like that, all of the patients. Unfortunately, we had to kill them all with shots to the head."

"When did this happen?"

"About a week ago."

"A week ago?" Sadie gave Ray an incredulous look. "And you're just now telling me?"

"I didn't want to tell you about a problem until we had a solution," Ray told her calmly.

"And what? You have a solution? Please tell me it's something other than shooting motherfuckas in the head!"

He reached deep inside of his pants pocket and pulled out a small syringe filled with a blue liquid. He held it up at eye level for both Sadie and Tyler to see.

"Our scientists were able to study the formula for VEM and create a serum that has the power to revert anybody from the high given from the drug. We took the drug off the market here, Say. I'm not selling that shit anymore *after seeing what the people turn into. We attracted everyone hooked on the drug here, with the promise of free VEM, this time an injected form. Hundreds of people showed up. The serum made them disoriented at first, and some passed out. But when they woke up, they were sober. Well, from VEM anyways."*

"How much of this stuff did they make?" Sadie asked, taking the syringe from him.

"A lot."

"Enough that we don't need any of the scientists any-more?" Sadie asked, and when Ray gave her a strange look, she said, "They know the formula to Vita E Morte.*"*

"What do you want to do with them?"

"What we have to," Sadie said coldly, and she knew Ray understood what she meant. "I want this lab de-stroyed. Is the original formula here?"

"No."

"Is it at your house?"

"Nope."

"Then where is it?" Sadie asked, growing tired of guessing.

"The safest place for it: Trap Street."

When Sadie stopped talking, Rhonnie and Ahli didn't seem shocked at all about what she had just told them. Neither did Cyril. The only thing they seemed interested in was the large backpack by her feet.

"This is the serum the scientists made." She reached inside the bag and pulled out a syringe. "We'll need to figure out a way to distribute it around the city and get it to our allies in other states."

"What's in that stuff?" Rhonnie asked

"I don't know, but it works. If you saw what I saw, you would understand how important this serum is."

"We know about the effects of VEM," Ahli admitted. "That's why Rhonnie and I took that time off in the first place. We got a test patient, because I wanted to show you firsthand why we couldn't keep selling that stuff."

She went on to tell Sadie about everything that had transpired up until that moment, from Jaq to his father, Angelo, and all the way to Crazy Tina. Hearing the complete story of VEM's origin sent a disturbance throughout Sadie's very being, mainly because she had seen what happened in the second stage personally.

"And we also went around and collected everybody's VEM. Gerron is dead by the way," Rhonnie quickly added to her statement. "We were trying to figure out a good way to tell you all of this, but hey, now we don't have to because you saw for yourself."

She gave Sadie a big, toothy smile, but Sadie's blank stare didn't falter.

"You went behind my back?" she asked, looking from Ahli to Rhonnie.

"We didn't want to, but we had to," Ahli told her. "You weren't listening to us."

"That still doesn't justify going behind my back."

"It should be the kind of thing you expect from me, since you need me to be spied on," Ahli shot back, and Sadie felt her mouth open slightly.

She closed it tightly and glanced at Rhonnie, who ducked to hide behind Cyril. Sadie took a deep breath in and let it out through her nose before addressing Ahli again. She wanted to say something boss-like, but the truth was she felt guilty.

"You didn't tell me how you really felt. And the last time someone close to me did that . . ." Her voice trailed off, and she felt Tyler watching her closely. She sighed. "The last time somebody did that, they broke my heart."

"Well, I'm not Mocha," Ahli said, shocking Sadie. "Anything I ever do will always be to help, never to hurt you. I would never turn on you, my family, for a man or anything else for that matter. But you not trusting me? That hurt *me*."

Sadie had never talked to either sister about her old best friend. She barely spoke her name, which was why she didn't understand how Ahli knew. "How . . ." Sadie's voice trailed off again.

"We've kind of been working *very* closely to you for a while now," Rhonnie said, coming back out from behind Cyril. "You tend to catch on to a few things. No matter how good a person tries to hide them."

"Well, I apologize if I hurt your feelings," Sadie told Ahli without pride. "I could have handled things in a better way. But that still doesn't justify you going around and calling shots without consulting me. If you don't hear from me, you wait. The Last Kings is a business that was built from the ground up. And some of these niggas don't play about their money. I'm glad Gerron was the only one who was killed."

"Okay, now that *that's* over and done with, can you elaborate on exactly what Trap Street is?" Rhonnie asked. "Is it some street with a bunch of trap houses?"

"Nah," Cyril spoke, not taking his eyes off Sadie. "It's a myth."

"People thought VEM was a myth," Sadie reminded him.

"Yeah, but Trap Street is a solid myth," Cyril said.

"I assure you it's not, kid," Tyler told him from beside Sadie. "But if you're not meant to know about it, then you don't."

"What do you know about Trap Street, Cyril? Humor me," Sadie inquired.

"Cane used to tell me about it when I was little. He said that it was a kingdom for the most elite hustlers, and only they would be told its location. It's a place where they hide all of their deepest, darkest secrets and most prized or priceless treasures."

"What else did he say?"

"That no matter the issue, it was a neutral ground for all hustlers. No blood could be spilled there, and if a person did commit an act of violence there, they would be removed from the earth forever."

"And do you know how he knew that?" Sadie asked.

"Shit, like any other story passed down, I guess. He couldn't have ever been the—" Sadie's sly smile cut him off, and he shook his head. "Nah."

But Sadie cleared his doubt with a nod. "How do you think we met?" Sadie asked. "Cane might not have been a kingpin, but he was elite. There aren't many like him, and you should be proud to have his blood coursing through your veins."

"Did he . . . did he put something there?" Cyril asked, and when Sadie nodded again, he leaned into the soft couch, mind blown.

Tyler's phone began to ring off the hook, and he left the sitting room to go answer it. Sadie didn't flinch. If it was his ex-fiancée, she hoped he was telling her, for the millionth time, to give it up and that he wasn't coming back. He was home.

"So, we have to go there?" Ahli asked. "To Trap Street?"

"Yes. I have to destroy the formula," Sadie told them. "And that's where it is."

"I'm coming."

"I'm coming too," Rhonnie pitched.

"Me three." Cyril threw up a hand.

At first, Sadie was going to tell them they couldn't come because they weren't elite, but as she looked at them, she felt a warmth come over her. If they weren't considered elite, then who was?

"All right, but we have to leave by morning," Sadie said and let her gaze fall on Cyril. "Why are you here anyways?"

"I asked him to come," Rhonnie said. "He thought you would be here to give him a refund on the VEM he ordered."

"And that's the only reason?" Sadie asked, remembering the scene she'd walked in on.

"That was the reason I came, but not the reason I stayed," Cyril answered and looked sweetly at Rhonnie.

Sadie had to admit, they were cute. And she was pleased with Rhonnie's choice in her man of interest. She hated Rhonnie and Tim together. He was beneath her. She didn't get much time to observe their interaction when she heard Tyler bellow from the other room.

"Fuck!" he shouted over and over, sending alarm throughout Sadie.

She jumped to her feet as he came back to the room, and she felt an unease come out of her when she looked in his eyes. There were tears there. She couldn't recall a time that she'd seen him cry, and before he told her what was wrong, she felt a sorrow come over her.

"Tyler, what's wrong?"

"I think you need to sit down before I tell you," he said, blinking his tears away.

"No, I'm not sitting down anywhere," she told him. "What happened?"

"Sadie—"

"Tyler! If you don't tell me what happened right now, I'm going to flip this damn house upside down."

"Somebody burned Grandma Rae's house down," he said, and Sadie felt her world shatter.

"W . . . what? Somebody did what?" Sadie's hand went shakily to her chest.

"I just got off the phone with Rashad. He said Evan never checked in when he was supposed to, so he went to see about it. He said everybody watching the block is dead. And the house is up in flames."

"No." Sadie began to sob uncontrollably and dropped to her knees.

Her body grew numb, and she couldn't even feel the ground under her. Grandma Rae's house was the only thing Sadie had left of the extraordinary woman. Losing her had been a turning point in Sadie's life, and Sadie had preserved the home in her memory. She'd taken some things out and moved them to a safe place, but for the most part, she'd left everything how it was. Everything about the home reminded Sadie about the woman who had raised her, from the aura to the smell of the walls. It was where the hustle in her was birthed, which was the only reason she had felt comfortable turning the basement into a stash spot. The neighborhood was one most people knew never to mess with. And now it was gone? Her grandmother's house was gone? How had it happened? She kept the block heavily guarded.

She felt like she was gasping for air and like the world had just gotten tiny. Both Ahli and Rhonnie came to comfort her. She felt their arms around her and their hands rubbing her back, but not even that made her feel better.

"Wait," Rhonnie said. "All the VEM was there. That's where we dropped it off."

The last sentence was barely out of her mouth when suddenly red lights began flashing throughout the mansion, and Sadie's security alarm sounded in a woman's voice. "Proximity alert! Proximity alert! The gate has been breached."

"What? What's going on? Rhonnie, did you try to override my security system again when I was gone?" Sadie snatched her phone out of her pocket to view the security footage of the gate.

She saw her guards at their usual posts, but when she zoomed in, she saw they weren't alive. They all had neat holes in their foreheads with blood trickling down. She switched cameras and saw two trucks coming up the drive toward the mansion.

"Oh, my God," she said and got to her feet.

"Who are they?" Ahli asked, looking at the phone.

"I don't know, but they murdered the guards at the gate. So they can't be here for anything good."

"Well, at least we know who hit your grandmother's house," Cyril said.

"Tyler, did Rashad say anything else?"

"Yeah, he said the woman who lives across from Grandma Rae's said she woke up when she heard noise outside. She didn't see anyone's face or much of what happened, but she did say she saw a man leave the house with a big black bag."

"The VEM," Rhonnie said. "We put it in a duffle bag."

"The VEM?" Sadie whispered, and she suddenly understood. "They're here for the formula."

"How do you know that?" Tyler asked.

"What else would it be?" Sadie said. "This is exactly what I thought would happen."

"How much time do we have?" Ahli asked.

"About five minutes before they get to the house. A few more for them to get inside."

"That's all we need. Come on, NaNa," she said as she and Rhonnie took off toward their bedroom quarters.

"Meet us in the basement in five minutes!" Sadie shouted after them and motioned for Tyler and Cyril to follow her.

She snatched up the bag with the serum in it and hurriedly led them to the basement of the mansion. Taking them to the gun range, she opened up a large locker that contained most of the firearms and weapons in the house.

"Damn, Say. It looks like you went shopping recently," Tyler said, noticing the new guns.

"Those are Rhonnie's and Ahli's. Here." She threw duffle bags at both Tyler and Cyril. "Load whatever you can carry."

The two of them instantly began filling their bags with artillery, vests, and ammunition. Sadie, not wanting to take any chances, hurried to fill three bags. But she wouldn't be able to carry them all when it was time to leave. She kept peeking over her shoulder, hoping to see Rhonnie and Ahli burst through the doors, but time was dwindling, and they still weren't there.

When she heard the loud commotion of her home being trashed, she knew the enemy had made it inside. The mansion was big, but it wouldn't take long for them to find their way to the basement.

"Sadie, we need to go," Tyler warned.

"Give it another minute," Sadie said and looked at the door of the gun range in a needy fashion. "They're gonna make it."

In the distance, she heard hurried footsteps, and she aimed an AK-47 at the doorway just in case. Relief came over her when she saw both sisters enter and in different sets of clothes.

"I wasn't going anywhere in those slippers. I needed some boots!" Rhonnie explained, seeing Sadie's thankful face.

"And I figured we would need this wherever we went." Ahli removed a backpack she wore and opened it, revealing heaps of cash.

"As long as you can carry it with these duffles. Here." Sadie handed them each a heavy duffle bag.

"How are we going to get out?" Ahli asked. "The only ways out are upstairs."

"That's what you think," Sadie said, going to one of the stalls and climbing over. "This house has a lot of secrets y'all don't know about. Come on."

Nobody questioned her as they jumped over the stall behind her. They ran on the action floor until they were behind the paper targets. Blended into the white wall, there was a door that nobody but Sadie knew was there. She pressed her thumb on a small sensor next to it, and with a soft beep, the door opened.

"Go, go, go!" She ushered them all inside a dimly lit tunnel before going through herself and closing the door tightly behind her. "We can't get to the garage attached to the house, not without going upstairs first. So we have to get a car from my other garage."

"Other garage?" Rhonnie and Ahli said in unison.

"Yes," Sadie said. "It's at the end of this tunnel."

"Always full of surprises," Tyler said in awe of his woman.

"Aren't you glad you called off your engagement?"

"Wait, you called off your engagement? Does that mean . . . Oh, my God! You're back together!" Rhonnie gushed.

"Not now, Rhonnie. We can talk about it later," Sadie said.

"I'm just saying, I hope so, because these last months, Sadie has been a real drag," Rhonnie added as they began to jog down the wide tunnel.

The second garage was half a mile away from the back of the house. When they got there, the only logical vehicle to take was an all-black Dodge Durango. They tossed the bags in the back of the truck, and when Sadie tried to get in the driver's seat, Tyler stopped her.

"I need you to be my shooter," he said. "Let me get us out of here."

"Okay," Sadie said and switched to the passenger's seat.

She clicked the garage door button on the visor in the truck, and when everyone was safely inside, they took off. She hit the garage button again and looked back as the door closed on her Ferrari and Lamborghini.

"All right, get ready," Tyler warned as he sped down the driveway that connected to the front drive.

The men rushing out of her home and back to their trucks didn't even notice the Durango speeding toward them until it was too late. Sadie waited until they were close enough to roll her window down and point the gun out. The moment they finally saw her was when she began to fire at will. The "ratatata" of the automatic weapon made them jump for cover, but her bullets invaded the bodies of most. She aimed for their tires and flattened all of them to ensure that nobody would follow the Durango. When they started to shoot back, she hurried to duck back in the car, and she rolled the window up. Their shots bounced right off the truck due to it being an armored vehicle, and they drove through the broken gate.

"Good shots, baby," Tyler said, leaning over and kissing her on the lips. "I just want to know how they found the address to your house, whoever they are."

"I know how," Rhonnie said from the back seat. "You're not going to like this, Sadie. But when I was running to the basement, I saw Jaq."

"Jaq?" Sadie asked and turned around in her seat. "The nigga who works for me?"

"It doesn't make any sense to me either," she said with a flustered face. "He was the one who refused to sell VEM. I don't know what he would be doing trying to steal it."

"It's the perfect cover," Cyril said. "You would have never thought of him to be one to cross you."

Sadie turned back around and gazed out the window at the dark road ahead of her. *First Cam, now Jaq.* Enough wasn't enough for anybody thirsting for the top spot. The car fell silent for several minutes.

"Where are we going? Are we driving to Trap Street?" Rhonnie asked, breaking the silence.

Tyler and Sadie laughed despite the seriousness of the situation.

"You don't drive to Trap Street," Sadie told her. "You fly."

Chapter 17

The water in the Jacuzzi was scorching hot on Olivette's skin, but she didn't wince. She welcomed the burn because it awakened all of her senses. The morning sun shone in on her through the open drapes of the large bathroom as she enjoyed her breakfast in the tub. She munched on strawberries while enjoying a glass of wine. It would have been a normal morning for her had it not been for Jeffrey's dead body sprawled out on the marble floor. His blood was still pouring out from the gash in his neck.

She didn't want to kill him, but she was one to only give one chance after a warning. Upon bringing her breakfast as she was getting ready to get in the tub, he made the mistake of clearing his throat at her again. She had no choice but to teach him a lesson, and it was just too bad that the lesson cost him his life. She'd stabbed him in the neck with the knife on her breakfast tray before wiping it off and using it to spread butter on her toast. She'd turned on her music to drown out the sound of him choking while he died so she could enjoy her food.

"Mmm," she said to herself, stuffing another strawberry into her mouth. "My garden has the best fruit!"

She hummed along to the soft R&B tunes playing in the background and rested the back of her head on the edge of the tub. Swallowing the piece of strawberry in her mouth, she closed her eyes and smiled. Olivette loved everything about her existence. Her life, her rules. She was the queen of her castle and every castle that surrounded her. The promise she'd made to herself long ago was one she held dear. No one would ever do anything around her that she didn't like. No one would speak to her in a way that she didn't care for. And anyone against her would face her fury. She was a beautiful woman who was capable of doing ugly things, and she had no remorse.

However, ever since Jaq had come to visit, she had been in a good mood. Not because of his sex, because Jaq's dick was mediocre, to say the least. But because of the news he'd brought her when he was there. Since his departure, she'd done every form of research on *Vita E Morte.* Everything about it engrossed her to the point where her fingers itched to have it in her grasp. The thought of running the drug game with a new drug excited her tremendously, especially with the knowledge of the power she would possess with it.

Jaq had strict instructions to get rid of Sadie and everyone else who could pose a threat. She'd even sent her best men to get the job done. Sadie wasn't as thorough as the stories about her had stated. She'd harbored a rat in her camp for over a year without noticing. Olivette would have snuffed him out ages ago. The thought of Sadie being a better drug lord than her was laughable. In fact, she found herself laughing out loud right then.

Her amusement was interrupted by her cell phone ringing on her golden food tray and making a loud and annoying sound. She was going to ignore the caller, but when she saw it was Jaq, she sat up quickly to answer it. She had high hopes that he had completed his mission.

"Jaq," she said, "I didn't think I would be hearing from you so soon. What is your news?"

"We got all of the VEM in the city that hasn't been sold yet."

"Perfect!" Olivette beamed at Jeffrey's body. "I assume that Sadie is dead as well."

"She's gone, ma'am," Jaq told her slowly.

"Even better! How did you murder her? A bullet to the skull? Slit her wrists?"

"No, ma'am. I mean . . . I mean she's *gone.*"

"Gone as in got away?" Olivette asked, wanting Jaq to clarify himself.

"Yes, ma'am. She got away when we tried to corner her inside her mansion. And, ma'am?"

"What!"

"She killed four of your men," Jaq said, giving her more bad news.

"And how the fuck did you let that happen?"

"She had an AK, ma'am. We didn't expect her to have such an advanced security system to alert her we were there."

"She's the head of a fucking cartel! Of course she has an advanced security system, you idiot!" Olivette fought the urge to throw her phone. "What's next? You're going to tell me that you didn't get the formula, too?"

"I'm sorry, ma'am. We couldn't find it. But we believe we know where it is."

"And how do you know that?"

"We were able to tap into the security footage inside of the house and listen to their conversation right before we got there."

"'Their' conversation? She wasn't alone?"

"No. She's with two men and two women. They were discussing where the formula is located. They want to destroy it."

"And where is that?"

"Someplace called Trap Street."

"Trap Street?" she repeated.

"Yes. Do you know where that is?"

Upon hearing the name, Olivette froze. She knew where it was all right. She was an elite. Of course that would be where something as rare as the formula of a drug like VEM would be hidden: the only place in the world where enemies could not fight or steal. It was the only pure place in the game, but Olivette had to have the drug, no matter what or where blood was spilled.

"Jaq?"

"Yes, ma'am?"

"How fast did you say VEM kicked in?"

"Almost instantly."

"And how fast does the stage where the user is all Hulk-like come?"

"I don't know. Maybe it depends on how many pills the person takes at once."

"I think we should test that theory. I want you and the rest of my men to get ready for a vacation."

"A vacation?"

"Yes. I'm taking you to the Caribbean."

Chapter 18

"It's hot!" Rhonnie complained when they got off the private plane.

"Shut up, NaNa," Ahli said, stepping out behind her sister. "Be thankful we still have our lives."

Rhonnie tried to keep her whining to a minimum, but it was really hot out. It was a different kind of heat than she'd ever experienced. She never thought that her first time out of the country would be because people were after them trying to kill them. But there they were, on the island of Antigua, surrounded by trees and water. It was the most beautiful thing she'd ever seen.

Sadie and Tyler walked ahead of everybody, and Rhonnie was doing her best to keep up, but Sadie had really stuffed the duffle bag she was toting.

"I'll take that," Cyril said, coming up behind her. He took the duffle bag from her and put it on his shoulder along with his.

"I could have carried that. It's heavy as hell. I don't want you pulling a muscle," she told him.

"I got it," he assured her. "You tryin'a call me weak?

"No. I know you aren't," she said, looking at his chocolate muscles.

The plane had landed them on a runway that had a few others in the distance. However, it wasn't attached to any airport. There was a truck not too far from them. When they got close enough, a tall man with dark skin and a face full of gray facial hair got out of the driver's seat. He wore a floral shirt and a big smile as he waved at them all.

"Sadie! Tyler! Welcome back!" he said when they reached them, and he opened his arms wide. "I wasn't expecting your call, but it's good to see you. And you brought friends!"

"Hey, Nathaniel," Sadie said and allowed Nathaniel to embrace her. "I didn't think I would be here today either, but you know my life."

"Always unpredictable," Nathaniel said with a grin. He turned to Tyler, and the two slapped hands. "How you doing, man?"

"Better now that I'm in this beautiful place with the woman I love."

"I heard that, man. Antigua is always beautiful this time of year. Come, I'll take you to where you'll be staying for the night. It will be dark soon, and I'm sure you want to rest after such a long flight. Especially since you have another long journey tomorrow."

"Yes, thank you, we would appreciate that very much."

Nathaniel helped Tyler and Cyril load their bags carefully in the back of the truck, and Rhonnie had a feeling that he knew exactly what was in them. She gently grabbed Sadie's elbow to get her attention before she could get in the vehicle.

"Trap Street isn't here?" she asked, thrown off by Nathaniel's words.

"No, it's on its own island. One that's not on any map. We have to travel there by boat."

"But, Sadie, I thought you said you fly to Trap Street."

"I guess I should have said you fly to the island closest to where Trap Street is. And then you travel by boat. You happy?" Sadie got into the back seat before Rhonnie could answer.

"Well, okay," Rhonnie mumbled to herself.

Sadie had been snippy ever since they'd left the mansion, and she had a feeling it had something to do with the fact that her grandmother's house had been burned down. Rhonnie tried to be understanding, especially since Sadie still hadn't had time to process it all. The moment she found out was the moment they had to start running, and there was no telling when all of it would be over.

The truck had three rows, so they all fit in comfortably. Rhonnie and Cyril sat beside each other in the very back. Sadie and Tyler sat next to each other in the middle row while Ahli sat in the front passenger's seat.

"Will there be a phone that I can use when we get to wherever we're going?" Ahli asked. "I know Brayland is going crazy with worry right now."

"Yes, but don't tell him where you are," Sadie warned.

"I'm just going to tell him I'm in Miami or something, don't worry," Ahli replied. "I just want to let him know I'm okay. Your boos are with you, so they don't have to worry about your well-being."

Rhonnie couldn't say that Cyril was her boo quite yet, but she could say that she'd never been on any kind of trip with a guy she liked. So that was saying something, even if they were only there to handle business. She looked out the window as they drove through the island, and she was even more in awe at the tall trees blowing in the breeze and the people enjoying their daily lives in such a pretty place. Just seeing how different the culture was elsewhere was amazing to her. She didn't even realize how big she was smiling until Cyril nudged her.

"First time out of the country?"

"Yeah," she answered, looking at him. "I always said I wanted to come, and I have a passport, obviously, but I just never made time to make the trip."

"Sometimes things happen to force us to do what we've always wanted."

"Here you go being all deep again," she teased.

"For real," he said seriously. "Your entire life is a design. The sooner you realize that, the more you'll appreciate it."

"A design, huh?"

"Yeah, a beautiful one." He used one of his fingers to stroke her cheek while his brown eyes were fixed on hers.

There they were. The butterflies had returned. Just as she thought she was getting used to his presence, another feeling of nervousness washed over her. How did he have that effect on her? His hand fell to hers, and he held it while stroking it with his thumb. Her head fell naturally on his shoulder and stayed there until they reached their destination.

"We're here, folks! The Sadie Inn in St. John's!" Nathaniel said and pulled in front of an elegant-looking building.

"The Sadie Inn?" Ahli asked.

"I donated some money to the island a while back, and they named a stay after me. It's no big deal," Sadie said modestly.

"No big deal?" Rhonnie said, peering out of her window. "This place looks almost as fancy as your house!"

"Come on, silly, I need a shower," Sadie said, rolling her eyes.

They unloaded from the truck and grabbed their things before making their way into Sadie Inn. The inside matched the outside with its gold and white theme.

Rhonnie felt like she was at Caesars Palace. As they checked in, Sadie looked at them all and spoke.

"I don't want Ahli to have to stay in a room by herself, so I think the girls should stay together and the boys should stay in a room together."

"I'm good with that," Tyler said.

"Yeah, that's cool," Cyril agreed.

"Okay, we will take two deluxe suites," Sadie said when she turned back to the desk clerk. "My name is Sadie Thomas."

"No problem," the older island woman checking them in said in a sweet tone. "It looks like you have a lifetime of free rooms, so there will be no charge today."

"Perfect. We also need clothes brought to our rooms," Sadie said and grabbed a piece of paper. She turned to Cyril and looked him up and down. "Rel, what are your sizes? Yours are the only ones I don't know."

When he told her, she wrote them down and handed the paper to the woman, who looked at it and nodded.

"I will take care of this right away. Here are your room keys. The suites are across the hall from one another. Enjoy your stay, Miss Thomas."

"Thank you."

Their rooms were on the third floor, and once they were there, Cyril and Tyler went their separate ways. When Rhonnie walked into the suite she would be sharing with Ahli and Sadie, she didn't think she would have to prepare herself.

"Oh, shit!" she exclaimed when she walked through the doors. "Look at the beds! Oh, my God, the rugs! That window seat! This looks like a scene from *Aladdin*. I feel like Princess Jasmine in this bitch."

"Why do you have to be so extra?" Ahli said, dropping her bags on the floor.

"The same reason you brought a bag of money we probably won't have to use," Rhonnie shot back.

Ahli didn't have a comeback, so instead, she just rolled her eyes. Sadie ignored both of them and headed for the bathroom immediately, not caring to shut the door as she stripped. The shower sounded, and Rhonnie heard a short and satisfied, "Ahhh!"

"Don't take all the hot water!" she said loud enough for Sadie to hear.

"The shower in here takes up half of the bathroom. It's big enough for all of us!" Sadie shouted back. "You better pretend we're in jail and get in, because I'm telling you now, I'm going to be in here for a while!"

Rhonnie didn't need to be told twice. She wanted to lie down but didn't want to get in the bed with the clothes she'd had on the entire flight. She and Ahli stripped out of what they were wearing and joined Sadie in the shower.

She was right. The shower was so huge that even if they stood with their arms extended, they wouldn't touch. The water spouted from all angles, and Rhonnie threw her head back as she got used to the sting on her body. Their backs were to each other as they bathed and relished the heat. Maybe it wasn't the perfect time to pick Sadie's mind, but there was never any better time than the present.

"You good, Sadie?" Rhonnie asked over her shoulder.

"You mean minus the fact that another one of my people turned against me, burned my grandmother's house down, stole my drugs, and broke into my home?"

"Well, since you put it that way, never mind. It was a stupid question," Rhonnie said.

"I'm sorry," Sadie sighed behind her. "It's not you, it's me. It just seems like whenever I gain something, I lose something. I got Tyler back, but then I lost my grandmother's house. Anything I get, I pay for it in pain. It's been like that since I can remember. I should be used to taking losses by now."

"That's not something anybody can get used to," Ahli voiced. "Not when your entire being relies on your wins."

"Yeah, don't be so hard on yourself, Say," Rhonnie said, calling Sadie by her nickname for the first time. "Sometimes shit happens that we can't control. Like Jaq. He's a snake-ass motherfucka, and his day of reckoning will come. Until then, we're here for a reason."

"No doubt," Ahli asserted. "And that's the most important thing."

"You're right," Sadie said, cheering up slightly. "I can't wait for you two to see Trap Street. It will change your life. Once you go one time, you're a part of it and it's a part of you forever."

Rhonnie finished showering, and when she got back to the room, she saw that someone had brought in a rack of clothing and several shoes for them. Cute items, too. However, all Rhonnie wanted to put on was some pajamas.

Right when she was about to just throw on one of the T-shirts and a clean pair of panties, there was a knock at the door. The other two were still in the bathroom, so she looked through the peephole to see who was there. She tightened the towel around her body and cracked the door open when she saw Cyril standing on the other side. He was wearing a nice silk V-neck and a pair of jeans.

"You in for the night?" he asked.

"Why do you ask?" She raised a brow.

"You want to spend your first night in another country in a hotel room?"

"I'm a little tired."

"Too tired to spend a few hours on the town with me?"

"Uhhh—"

"She's coming as soon as she gets dressed!" Ahli's voice said loudly.

Rhonnie glared at her sister over her shoulder, but Ahli just gave an annoying grin. She turned back to Cyril and shrugged. "I guess I'll be out as soon as I get dressed."

"Good shit. I'll wait for you by the front desk."

"Okay," Rhonnie said and shut the door. She whipped back around to face her sister. "Why did you just do that?"

"Because you don't just like him, you *really* like him, duh," Ahli answered with a neck roll.

"Who was that?" Sadie asked, poking her head out of the bathroom.

"Cyril. He wants to take Rhonnie out, and she's acting like she doesn't want to go."

"You don't want to go?" Sadie directed her gaze at Rhonnie.

"I never said I don't want to go," Rhonnie said, exasperated. "I just . . . Cyril makes me feel all weird inside."

"It might be love," Sadie noted, wagging a finger.

"Love! I just met him."

"So?" both Sadie and Ahli said together.

"What do you mean 'so'?"

"Rhonnie, let me be the first to tell you that you can't put a time limit on what you feel for someone," Sadie said, schooling her. "Sometimes you can fall in love overnight, but getting to know that person is how you decide if you stay in love. You know, Tyler and I had our first date by accident in Jamaica."

"And look, they're still together," Ahli hinted. "And look at me and Bray. Fate put us together. I love him more than life itself. Who knows? Cyril could be your Tyler or Brayland, but you won't know if you don't go."

"So go!" Sadie shouted and wrapped a towel around her own body. "Let's see what goodies they brought up here for you."

For the next twenty minutes of her life, Rhonnie felt like a life-sized Barbie. Between Ahli braiding her hair into two braids and Sadie making her try on outfit after outfit, she was over the date before it even started. However, when she saw her reflection in the end, she had to admit that they did a good job. She wore a black dress that wasn't too tight or too loose. It stopped at her mid-thigh and showed off her thick, muscular legs. On her feet, she wore a pair of brown flat sandals that matched one of the crossbody purses that was also on the rack.

"Here, before you go, since we didn't have time to convert our money," Sadie said and went to one of the golden dressers in the room. She opened the top drawer and revealed stacks of Eastern Caribbean dollars. She grabbed a stack and handed it to Rhonnie. "I'm sure Tyler showed Rel where the currency is in their room. But a lady should always have her own bag."

"Thank you," Rhonnie said and waved at them before she left. "Wish me luck."

"Luck!" they both shouted as the door closed.

Rhonnie made her way to the first level, and she worried that she'd taken too long. She hoped he hadn't gotten tired of waiting for her and gone back to his room. But when she rounded the corner of the hallway, she found Cyril sitting patiently on one of the chairs. When he saw her, his face lit up, and it made her cheeks grow warm. He stood up and extended a single rose to her when she approached him.

"Thank you," she said, taking the rose and smelling it.

"You're welcome, shorty. I guess tonight my favorite color is black." He jokingly licked his lips at her, and she giggled.

"Is that right?"

"Hell yeah. I wish I were that dress so you could wear me like that."

"Oh, my God! Stop it!" Rhonnie said, laughing loudly.

"My bad. I get like this when I'm in the presence of greatness," he said and extended his arm. "Let's go before we miss all the fun. You hungry?"

"Starving."

He took her out to the busy street and led her through the crowds of people. He maneuvered them so well that she wondered if he'd been to Antigua before. She hoped that he didn't want to try something new and different to eat. Her stomach was too hungry to be testing out new cuisines. All she wanted was a nice, greasy burger and fries or some chicken, so she was happy when they found an American restaurant. They sat at a table outside, and the waitress came quickly with their drinks and food orders. Cyril dived right into his food, but Rhonnie paused before taking a bite out of her burger to observe him.

"You've been here before, haven't you?" she asked.

"What makes you say that?"

"Because the way you navigated through those people, it just seemed like you knew where you were going."

"Nah. I was just following the wave of the crowd," he admitted. "I've never been here before, but I'm happy my first time is with you."

"There you go again."

"There I go doing what?" he feigned innocence, but Rhonnie pursed her lips at him.

"You know what I'm talking about."

"Tell me."

"You keep doing that flattery thing."

"I'm being real, though. I fuck with you. You're different, and I like it. I feel like I can be my complete self when I'm around you because you get it. You get *me*. Ain't no faking."

"What's crazy is that I feel the same way," Rhonnie told him. "Well, kind of. I'm usually so confident, but when I'm with you? I feel like a shy little girl."

"Is that a bad thing?" he asked, and she pondered the question for a moment.

"At first I thought it was."

"And now?"

"Now it just feels good to not be a hard ass all the time." She shrugged. "Working for Sadie means that I have a mug on my face eighty percent of the time. I can't show emotion. So I guess I like that you remind me that I have feelings and that I'm a woman before a soldier."

"I like how you just said that," he told her. "Do you see yourself doing what you do for a while?"

"Yes," she answered honestly. "I like my job. What about you?"

"I plan on getting out of the game eventually. But I just got started, so I don't see the end anytime soon unless one of these niggas puts me in an early grave."

"Don't say stuff like that," Rhonnie told him with a disapproving face.

"That's the game, though." He shrugged and took a sip of his strawberry lemonade. "I've seen it up close. The difference between me and these other niggas is that I know I'm not invincible. I know my time gon' be up someday, so while I'm here, I just try to make the best of it. I want every day to count and go toward something."

"Ain't nobody putting you in the earth anytime soon so long as I have something to say about it," Rhonnie said matter-of-factly. "You're not just the nigga I like. You're family now. We protect each other."

The sad look that he gave her almost made her feel that she'd said something to offend him. But when he took her hands in his and brought them to his soft lips, she knew everything was all right. She realized that the look in his eyes wasn't one of sadness. It was one of sincerity.

"What?" she asked.

"I can't look at you?" He countered her question with one of his own and kissed her knuckles again.

"I don't care. But if you stare too hard, you'll start to notice my flaws."

"Girl, you trippin'. Ain't no flaws in what I'm looking at."

"Yeah, yeah. You're going to see that one of my eyes is a tiny bit bigger than the other in a second."

"Now that you mention it . . ." Cyril joked.

"You play all day, don't you?"

"The same as you. If there's one thing I've noticed about you, shorty, it's that you can make light of any situation, no matter how grave."

Rhonnie retracted her hands and began to eat the fries on her plate. He was right. Rhonnie could crack jokes all day. It was her way of coping with the things around her. They finished their food while having more conversation, and by the time it was over, Rhonnie's cheeks hurt from smiling so much. When they left the restaurant, they did more sightseeing, and somehow Cyril talked her into doing nighttime ziplining in a dress, which turned out to be a blast.

When they finally got back to the Sadie Inn, Cyril and Rhonnie stood closely facing each other in the hallway that separated their two rooms. She had a natural high coursing through her and wished that the night didn't have to end, but they had things to do in the morning. Things that they needed to be well-rested for, so she accepted the fact that he had to go.

"Good night," she told him and gave a happy sigh. "I don't remember the last time I had this much fun. Thank you for that."

"No problem. I wouldn't mind doing that all the time."

"What, ziplining at night?"

"Nah, making you smile," he said, and she felt her knees grow weak.

She wrapped her arms around his neck so that she wouldn't fall, and when she looked up, she realized she was right where she needed to be. He placed his hands on the small of her back and brought her even closer to him before giving her his parting gift. Their lips connected, and when Rhonnie closed her eyes, she swore she saw fireworks of passion. She'd wondered before if his lips were soft. Well, now she knew. They were the softest she'd ever felt on hers, and she couldn't help slipping her tongue through them. They kissed each other as if they were long-lost lovers just now finding each other again. When they finally broke the kiss, she lowered her eyes at him in wonder. Slightly stumbling, she stepped away from him to go inside her suite. Not because she wanted to, but if she didn't, she was afraid of what she might do. It wasn't just her body that wanted him. Her mind did too.

"I'll see you in the morning," Cyril said, backing up to his room door as well.

"Okay," she said, pulling out the room key from her bag. "See you in the morning."

She opened the door and went through, but not without looking over her shoulder and seeing that he was staring back at her. She held up her hand and waved with her fingers before shutting the door. Ahli and Sadie were already sleeping, so she would have to tell them about her night in the morning. She took off the dress and put on a T-shirt before climbing in the bed with her sister. Sleep crept up on her faster than she expected, but when it found her, she was thinking one last thought.

Maybe Cyril had been right. Maybe her life was a design and everything that had happened had brought her to exactly where she was supposed to be. Maybe.

Chapter 19

Things moved quickly the next morning. As soon
as the sun was shining in the beautiful clear skies above,
they were on their way to the ocean. Sadie had told them
that Trap Street was located on an unnamed island a little
ways away from Antigua, and the only way there was by
boat. Ahli knew that, but that still didn't make her ready
for the trip.

While everyone else was chatting it up on the chartered boat, she sat alone, telling herself that it would all
be over soon. She was also the only one with a life jacket,
which she personally insisted on wearing. She could
swim, but she wasn't the best at it. If the boat overturned,
she just wanted to be prepared. She could acknowledge
how pretty the water looked, but still, she couldn't forget
what kinds of monsters lurked in it.

"I don't think I've ever seen you look so uptight
before," Sadie's voice sounded loudly over the wind.

She looked up and saw everyone staring at her with
amusement on their faces. "I've been in more battles than
I can count, but this is a different vibe," Ahli admitted.
"I've never fought off a great white shark."

"Shark attacks are rare, but if it does happen . . ." Sadie
pointed at the bags of guns they'd brought.

"Let's just pray it doesn't," said Ahli.

The journey to the island was about an hour long, an hour too long if you let Ahli tell it. In her mind, she imagined the island to be a desolate place. Nothing like Antigua, which had been slightly modernized since it was such a tourist attraction. She imagined it being like Gilligan's Island and them having to fend for themselves against the jungle. Boy, was she wrong.

Nathaniel pulled the boat up to a dock, and Ahli noticed the other, fancier boats there. The shore was clear, and there were many trees around, but not so many to resemble a forest. In fact, there was a road and buildings all over, much like Antigua. The only thing was it was quiet. It looked as if people inhabited the island, except there was nobody there. She waited until the boat was completely stopped to take off her life jacket and grab her things.

"Come," Nathaniel said and gestured for them to follow him onto the wooden dock. When they were all unloaded, Ahli noticed that he didn't step away from the boat. "This is as far as I am permitted to go. I will be back to get you all at sunset. Take these."

From his pocket, he pulled out a set of keys, then pointed to an armored Hummer in the distance. Sadie took them and nodded in thanks. The five of them walked up the dock, and Ahli tried to get a better look at the boats that were there. She found herself wondering how long they had been sitting there.

"Those are the boats of guests on the island," Sadie said, reading her mind as they walked side by side.

"Who fills the tanks?" Ahli asked.

"The Keepers of the island," Sadie said.

"Have you ever seen them?"

"Nobody has. They say they only show their faces when the rules are broken," Sadie answered. "And I've never broken the rules or know anybody who has. So I'm sure you get where I'm going with that."

"Mystical," Rhonnie said, coming up on them. "What do they call this island?"

"It has no real name, but we call it Hustle Island."

"Hustle Island? I like that," Rhonnie poked her bottom lip out slightly and nodded in approval. "Is it always this quiet?"

"Always," Sadie told her. "People come here for peace. They come here when they need to get away from chaos for a while."

"What about you?"

"I come and do what I do everywhere else: handle my business. I never stay anywhere too long."

They reached the truck and got in. Ahli sat comfortably in the back with Rhonnie and Cyril, and as they drove, she found herself sneaking peeks at them. Rhonnie had told her all about her night with him, and Ahli was glad that her sister had found a little happiness in their unpredictable lives. And from the looks of it, Cyril really liked her, too. The way he looked at her sister reminded her of someone she knew. Ahli had told Brayland that she was on a business trip with Sadie, and he didn't question it, but she couldn't wait to get back and see him.

They rode in silence as Sadie navigated them on a narrow road through a town. They passed many vacant buildings, and Ahli kept waiting for them to see another person. However, that never happened. After driving for about ten minutes, Ahli saw what looked to be a tall gate. It was thick, like one used to guard a castle. Sadie slowed to a stop when they got to it and glanced in the rearview mirror at the three of them.

"Get out," she instructed as she opened her door.

Ahli didn't understand, but the encouraging smile Tyler gave her from the front seat made her listen. She got out and went to where Sadie stood by a wall next to the gate. Like the wall in the gun range, there was a finger sensor. Except the one by the gate seemed more advanced, and the screen was bigger. Sadie pressed her finger on it, and the entire thing lit up.

"Welcome back, Sadie Thomas," a computerized voice said.

"I brought friends," Sadie stated to the sensor.

"Checking authorization limits," the computer voice said, and a second later, the screen turned green. "Authorization status: active and limitless. Please have the person or persons press their thumb on the sensor pad."

Sadie extended an arm to Ahli and waved for her to step forward. Slowly, Ahli approached the sensor and put her thumb on it. The screen lit up again.

"Please state your first and last name," the computer said.

"Ahli Malone."

"Ahli Malone. Status: active and limited," the voice stated.

"What does that mean?" Ahli asked Sadie when she took her finger back.

"It means you now have access to Trap Street. However, you cannot ever bring anyone with you who is not an elite."

"But you can?"

"Yes."

After Sadie did the same thing for Rhonnie and Cyril, she instructed the gate to open, and they got back in the truck. The gate was slow to rise, and Ahli leaned forward in anticipation. When it was all the way up, her eyes almost bulged out of her head. And from the sounds of it, Cyril and Rhonnie were having the same reactions beside her.

"Wow," Ahli breathed.

"Welcome to Trap Street," Sadie said, echoing the sign they passed when they drove through the gate.

The gate closed again, but Ahli was too busy looking forward and not back. Trap Street was nothing like what Ahli had assumed. It wasn't a bunch of trap houses lined up on a block, nor was it a run-down place. If she hadn't known they were on an island far away from everything else, Ahli might have guessed that she was in Beverly Hills. Except, instead of multiple mansions, there were only four, two on either side of the street. They each took up so much land that it seemed as if the street ran forever.

"There are four Houses," Tyler explained. "Greed, Power, Prosperity, and Divinity."

"So, you're separated by the kind of hustler you are?" Cyril asked.

"Correct. The island's Keepers place you in the House that best suits you."

"But how can they place you if they don't know anything about you?" Rhonnie asked.

"You already gave them everything they need to know," Tyler said and held up his thumb. "No matter how far off the grid you might think you are, they find out everything about you, even your darkest secrets."

"What House are you in?" Rhonnie asked.

"Prosperity," he answered.

"What about you, Sadie?" she asked.

"Divinity," Sadie answered.

"Me and Ahli are probably in Greed," she joked.

"We'll know soon enough," Sadie said simply, driving by the first two Houses. "Ty, do you need to stop by your room at all?"

"Nah," he answered, looking around. "I honestly want to do what we came to do and leave. I wonder where everyone is at."

"Probably in their rooms," Sadie said. "It is still kind of early."

She drove down the remainder of the street until they got to an all-white mansion, the Divinity House. It had to have been at least 20,000 square feet and one of the biggest houses Ahli had seen. Sadie parked in the circled drive, and they all got out of the car that time. Ahli left her bag in the car, figuring she wouldn't need weapons, though Rhonnie carried her bag inside.

When they got inside, the openness of the foyer made Ahli spin around with her arms wide. She felt a welcoming sensation come over her the moment she walked through the doors. The place seemed familiar to her, although she'd never been there before. There was what looked to be a check-in desk right as soon as they came through the doors, but nobody was there.

"That's weird," Sadie said to herself, but Ahli heard it. "Benji is always here."

Ahli stopped spinning and watched her boss approach the desk. As soon as she got there, though, a man popped up out of seemingly nowhere. He was of average height and looked to be of mixed Caribbean ethnicity. He was in his mid to late thirties and had a head full of soft, curly hair. He was dressed like a bellhop with a tiny hat on top of his head. His eyes brushed over everyone until they finally fell on Sadie.

"Sadie!" he said with a smile. "For some reason, I was expecting you."

"Were you?" she said and gave him a curious look.

"Yes," he said, holding up three pieces of paper. "You approved new members, I see. We haven't had anyone new in years. I hope they fit the bill for this place."

"That and then some," she told him. "Benji, this is Ahli, her sister Rhonnie, and Cyril Anderson."

"Anderson?" Benji's eyes fell on Cyril and studied him. "Would you, by chance, be related to a Cane Anderson?"

"He was my older brother," Cyril answered, and Benji gave him a look of condolence.

"Ahhh, it makes sense then," Benji said, handing him a piece of paper and a key.

"What makes sense?"

"That you were placed in the House of Prosperity, same as your brother. That is the key to his room, now yours. I was deeply saddened to hear about his departure from this earth, but I am sure you will keep his belongings safe, as well as add a few things of your own."

"Thank you," Cyril told Benji.

Ahli peeked at the piece of paper in his hands and saw that it had his name under the word "Prosperity," as well as a room number.

"Rhonnie, you too are in the House of Prosperity," Benji said, handing her a piece of paper and a key.

"Prosperity?" Rhonnie seemed truly shocked. "I thought I would be in Greed."

"The decision to house you accordingly isn't solely based on the things you've done," Benji explained. "It ultimately comes down to your heart and the path you're taking to the future. The Keepers of this island must see something prosperous in you, young lady. Lastly, we have the most curious of all. Ahli, is it?"

"Yes, that's me."

"You, my dear, have been placed in the House of Divinity," he said.

Sadie looked shocked, but not more shocked than Benji. As he handed her the piece of paper and her key, he eyed her peculiarly, as if he were trying to figure her out. Ahli looked from Sadie and back to Benji, not understanding why they were looking at her like she was an alien.

"I don't get it. What's the big deal?" she asked.

"In all the decades of this place being here, only five before you have ever been placed in the House of Divinity," Benji told her.

"I was the fifth," Sadie told her.

"Making you the sixth," Benji continued. "In fact, up until today, Sadie has been the only living soul housed in Divinity."

"Until now," Sadie said, still giving Ahli an odd look.

"Well, before I let you go, I should inform the newcomers of the rules we require all of our houseguests to follow," Benji said, looking at Rhonnie, Ahli, and Cyril. "This is neutral ground, which means that committing crimes by any means will not be tolerated. There will be no fighting, and murder is punishable by death."

"Well, how ironic. If you break the rule for killing somebody, you get killed," Rhonnie stated.

"Correct," Benji told her with a smile.

"So we shouldn't have these guns then?" she asked, lifting up her bag.

"By all means, you can bring whatever you like inside. I would just advise you against using weapons of any kind while here. Because this is—"

"Neutral ground," Rhonnie told him. "I heard you."

With that, Benji left them to do only God knew what. As Ahli looked down at the piece of paper, she couldn't help but wonder how background checks had been done so quickly. It wasn't that long of a drive from the gate to the Divinity House. She also wondered what about her had made them place her in the rarest House of all.

"I'm about to go do what I came here to do," Sadie told them. "Tyler, will you show Rhonnie and Cyril around the Prosperity House?"

"No problem," Tyler said and gestured for them to follow him.

When they were gone, Sadie turned to Ahli. "You follow me."

"Okay."

Ahli walked closely behind Sadie up the U-shaped staircase to a set of elevators. The doors opened the moment Sadie pressed the button, and the two of them boarded in silence. Ahli couldn't tell if Sadie was angry at her House placement, but it was obvious that she felt something about it. When they reached the third floor, Sadie stepped out first and waited for Ahli to come behind her.

"Let me see your paper." Sadie held her hand out, and Ahli gave it to her. "Room 380. That's right across from mine. Good. That means we won't have to go all around this place looking for it. If you think you can get lost in my mansion, try moving around the Divinity House. This way."

They began a journey down a well-lit corridor. It smelled fresh, like someone had just come through and cleaned it. They passed many doors but stopped at none. Ahli looked at the number above one of the rooms and saw that they were only at room 330. They still had a long way to go.

"I don't get it," Ahli said, breaking their awkward silence as they walked.

"Get what?"

"Why I was placed in this House if it's a rarity."

"I wondered the same thing too for a while, about myself," Sadie admitted. "But then I stopped because I realized that this is where I belong. I feel a kind of peace in this House that I've never felt before. Not even Tyler can make me feel as safe as this House makes me feel. And you feel that same way too, don't you? I saw it the second you walked in, how free you became."

"I did," Ahli said, thinking back to the calming feeling that washed over her when she stepped into the House.

"For the Keepers to have placed you here, they had to have felt that you are touched by God."

"Touched by God? After everything I've done?"

"Some things aren't meant for us to understand. Sometimes we're just meant to accept them."

Sadie stopped abruptly, and before Ahli could question why, she realized they'd reached their destination. Room 380. The door in front of them was made out of solid gold. She glanced down at the key in her hand before putting it in the keyhole and turning it. When she heard the door unlock, she turned the knob and pushed the door open.

She didn't know what she had expected. Maybe she thought it would be filled with riches. But when she saw that it was no different from a luxury hotel suite, with a living room area and bedroom in the back, she was outwardly disappointed.

"The room is what the key holder makes of it," Sadie said, taking notice of the look on Ahli's face. "There are no treasures because you haven't stored any here yet.

Give it time. Soon it will be filled with the things that make your heart sing."

Ahli nodded and closed the door. "Okay, let's do what we came here to do," she said, and the two stepped across the hall and into Sadie's room.

Sadie's room was the complete opposite of Ahli's. It was filled with things of wonder, things that Ahli was sure Sadie had accumulated over the years, some new, some old. Sadie took Ahli to her bedroom, and Ahli was shocked to see the dated bedroom furniture. However, Sadie walked up to one of the chests of drawers and ran her hand across the top of it lovingly. A sad smile came to her lips, and she inhaled deeply. Ahli looked closely at the room and at the photos hanging in frames on the wall. She noticed that a little girl in a few of the photos closely resembled Sadie.

"This was my grandma Rae's stuff," she confessed to Ahli. "Almost everything in this bedroom. I set my room here up exactly as she had it in her room, all the way down to the quilt folded at the end of that bed. And this!" She gave a light laugh of joy and picked up a small photo album that was on top of the dresser. "These were all her favorite pictures of us all when Ray and I were little. Everything in my room here at the Divinity House is priceless. This stuff might not be worth much to anyone else, but to me, it is equivalent to millions. I would die to protect these things."

And Ahli knew that she meant it. Sadie moved on to a wooden jewelry cabinet in the room. She stared at it for a few moments before opening it. At first, Ahli thought she was actually going to look at jewelry until she pulled out a thick piece of folded-up paper. Ahli didn't need to guess what it was, because it was the same piece of paper she'd retrieved from her mother's piano to give Sadie three years ago. It was the formula to *Vita E Morte.*

"Ray asked Benji to put it somewhere I would know to find it."

"In a jewelry box?"

"Yes," Sadie said, peering down at the parchment. "My grandmother always said that when thieves go into a jewelry box, they're only looking for jewels. Not the things that hold more value than money."

"Your grandmother sounded like a wise woman."

"She was," Sadie said fondly before tucking the formula into her seemingly heavy backpack. "I'm done here for now. We can go."

"Are you going to burn it?" Ahli asked when they left the room.

"No. I want to tie it to a rock and let it go into the ocean," Sadie said, locking the door.

By the time they made it back outside, they saw that the others hadn't made it back yet. They decided to wait by the car until Rhonnie, Cyril, and Tyler showed back up. Ahli didn't know why, but suddenly she felt an eerie feeling around her. It made sense why the Divinity House was so desolate, but as she looked around, she didn't see anybody else. That was strange, because she had seen the boats, so she knew people were there.

"Sadie, are you sure it's always this quiet?" Ahli asked.

"Yes," Sadie said, glancing around.

"But it's not just quiet. It seems empty."

"Like nobody is here. I get what you mean." Sadie looked at the other Houses in the distance. "I wonder where everyone is."

"Let's go ask Benji."

"Good idea."

They went back inside to Divinity House and rang the bell on the front desk since Benji wasn't there. It sounded throughout the whole House so a person could hear it no matter where they were. The two of them waited a good five minutes, but still, nobody showed up.

"I'm going to try to call to the other Houses," Sadie said and went around the counter.

As soon as she rounded it, however, an uneasy look came over her face. Her eyes were on something on the ground, and she didn't say a thing. Her expression prompted Ahli to join her on the other side of the counter, and soon she saw why Ahli was looking like that. Now they knew why Benji wasn't answering the bell. He was dead. The man Ahli had just met not too long ago was lying facedown in a pool of his own blood.

"What the fuck?" Sadie said in a low tone, bending down to check his pulse. "He's dead. His neck is slit. Somebody else is here. We have to go, now!"

She and Ahli ran out of the house and got in the Hummer to meet the others at the Prosperity House. Sadie sped down Trap Street, but when someone stepped in the road, she pressed hard on the brakes, causing them to lurch forward.

A young woman with skin so fair that she looked almost white blocked their path. She was wearing a black skintight jumpsuit and a pair of boots, despite the warm weather. Her long ombre hair blew in the wind, and if it weren't for the evil expression on her face, she would have been pretty. Ahli had never seen her, and from the looks of it, Sadie didn't know who she was either. However, when Jaq and several others stepped out into the road on either side of her, with big guns pointed at the truck, Ahli understood.

"They found us. They're here for the formula."

"No shit," Sadie said. "I'm not giving it to them."

"Sadie!" the woman in the street called. "Sadie Thomas! Head of The Last Kings cartel, step out of the car."

"Is this car bulletproof?" Ahli asked, thinking that maybe they could drive right through them.

"I don't know," Sadie admitted. "What reason would it have to be? Nobody is supposed to use guns here."

"Well, if they're going to play dirty, then I am too," Ahli said, pulling an M16 out of one of the bags.

"No! We're on sacred ground. We can't fight here," Sadie said adamantly.

"Tell that to Benji," Ahli said, loading the gun with a drum. "My job is to protect you at all costs. So if my membership in this little club gets revoked, so be it."

"Sadie! I know you can hear me. Step out of the vehicle and I'll let your friend live," the woman in the street called.

Ahli kept getting her weapons ready, but when she looked up at Sadie, she already knew what she was about to do. She took the backpack off and handed it to Ahli, who was shaking her head feverishly.

"Find the others," Sadie instructed.

"I won't leave you. Sadie, don—"

But it was too late. Sadie had already stepped out.

"Fuck!" Ahli shouted and climbed over to the driver's seat.

She was conflicted, so she didn't drive off right away. She watched the woman smile sickly as Sadie approached her fearlessly. Ahli cracked the window open so that she could hear what was being said. She couldn't see Sadie's face since her back was to the truck, but she could hear her voice.

"You wanted me? Here I am," Sadie said, stopping in front of the woman. "To what do I owe this pleasure?"

"You know why I'm here," the woman said.

"How could I know that when I don't even know who you are?"

"How rude of me." The woman feigned a giggle. "My name is Olivette Jenkins."

"Olivette Jenkins? You run an operation out of Puerto Rico now, don't you?"

"New Mexico and a few other states," Olivette corrected with a sneer.

"Forgive me if I don't keep track of the people under me," Sadie told her innocently. "How did you get in here?"

"Because, like you, I'm an elite." Olivette pursed her lips and shrugged her shoulders. "Surprise!"

"Let me guess. You were housed in Greed."

"Wrong. Power."

"That would have been my second guess. If you know the location of Trap Street, then you know the rules on this island, don't you?"

"Do I look like someone who gives a fuck about *rules?*" Olivette laughed. "Do you think I've gotten this far by following rules? Ask my parents. Oh, wait. You can't. I killed them, oops. Just like I killed everyone else who was here before your arrival. You don't understand the joy I felt when I saw that Hummer drive through here."

"You're sick."

"No, I'm a woman who will do anything to be in charge. Even break some fake-ass rules just to keep people like you and me in line. Now enough small talk. Where is the formula?"

"What formula?" Sadie asked, still playing dumb.

"For *Vita E Morte!* You know what the fuck I'm talking about. I know you have it."

"Oh, that formula. I destroyed it already," Sadie said with a shrug.

"You lie," Olivette said and searched Sadie's face.

"Maybe I am, maybe I'm not."

"Don't patronize me, bitch!" Olivette shouted and backhanded Sadie so hard that her head snapped to the side.

That was all Ahli needed to see. She grabbed the M16 and jumped out of the vehicle.

"Lay another hand on her and I'll turn your body into noodles," she said, aiming the gun at Olivette.

"I told you to leave, Ahli," Sadie said through clenched teeth.

"And I told you I wasn't going to."

"Oh, how cute. You brought a mutt with you," Olivette taunted and then beamed at Jaq. "I brought mine with me too."

"And that's a pity," Sadie said, spitting blood on the pavement. "You would have moved up in the ranks nicely, Jaq."

Jaq spat viciously at Sadie's feet, and it was that action alone that made Ahli look closely at him. She had never known him to be so ferocious with his movements. The look in his eyes was different, but there was something in them that she recollected. His pupils dilated, making his eyes seem darker than they naturally were. Way darker. Suddenly she realized where she recognized them from.

Crazy Tina had the same kind of eyes when she was doped up on VEM.

Suddenly, Ahli looked at everyone Olivette had with her. They had the same look in their eyes. She gasped.

"Sadie!" she exclaimed, and Sadie glanced back at her briefly. "They're high on VEM."

The word seemed to be a trigger for Olivette's soldiers, because suddenly they bared their teeth and dropped their guns. They crouched low and held their hands out like claws, making them all look like animals ready to pounce.

"Your mutt has good eyes," Olivette said and then pet Jaq on the head. "See Jaq told me all about what VEM can do, so I sent him to steal all of what you had."

"But that wasn't even two days ago," Ahli said, looking at the soldiers who were well into the second stage of the drug. "It looks like they've been using for a while."

"I guess that's what happens when you take four pills at a time." Olivette giggled again like a happy schoolgirl. "These motherfuckas are strong, and it's going to take more than that M16 to put them down. And as long as I give them what they want, they'll do whatever I say. Ain't that right, Jaq Bear?"

Jaq sneered as a response.

"With a drug like *Vita E Morte,* I'll be able to control not only the drug game, but the world. I'll have the president of the United States eating grapes out of my asshole. There would be nobody more powerful than me, and that makes this drug imperative to me. Now, where's the formula!" Olivette shouted at the top of her lungs.

In response, Sadie spat in her face, and then it was as if she and Ahli shared one mind. They both ran toward the truck at the same moment. Sadie got back in the driver's seat, and Ahli got in the passenger's.

"Get them!" Olivette screamed, and her soldiers took off toward the truck.

Ahli rolled her window down and raised her gun to fire, but Sadie swiped it down right before she could get a shot off.

"No blood will be on our hands here," she told Ahli and sped off. Some of the soldiers tried to jump on the front of the car, but Sadie was able to shake them off. "This island is—"

"Sacred, I know!" Ahli finished for her in an irritated tone.

"There's only one way in and one way out of Trap Street!" Olivette shouted in their dust. "Run and hide all you want. But I will find you. And I *will* get what I came for."

Ahli turned around and saw the soldiers running faster than what she thought was humanly possible after the truck, but they still weren't fast enough to keep up. Soon, Ahli couldn't see any of them anymore.

Sadie pulled the truck in front of the Prosperity House just as Rhonnie, Tyler, and Cyril were coming out of it. Tyler's alarmed eyes went straight to the blood on Sadie's lips.

"What happened?" he asked, walking up to the car window.

"They found us," Sadie told him. "Jaq has been working for some bitch named Olivette Jenkins this whole time."

"The one who runs an operation in Puerto Rico?"

"New Mexico," Sadie and Ahli corrected him at the same time.

"How the fuck did she get in here?" Rhonnie asked.

"She's an elite, her House is Power, she killed Benji, and she brought her own small army. And did I mention that they're all doped up on VEM?" Ahli's words came out quickly.

"She killed Benji? I thought that was against the rules."

"She doesn't care. She killed all the other elites who were here. That's why it's vacant," Sadie said. "She'll do anything to get this formula."

"Do you have it?" Cyril asked.

"It's in my bag in here with us."

"Then why haven't you destroyed it yet? Just burn that bitch!" Cyril said like it was simple.

"She can't," Tyler said, giving Sadie a look of understanding.

"Why can't she?" Rhonnie asked. "I'm sure there's a lighter somewhere in the car."

"No, I mean, she *can't.*"

"It's one of the rules, isn't it?" Ahli asked, and Sadie nodded.

"You can't set anything to flame. Ray knew what he was doing by bringing the formula here," Sadie said and briefly looked directly at Cyril. "Anything stored here can never leave again. And in order to destroy something you don't want anymore, you must do it definitively. You have to send it to the deepest part of the earth no man has ever been."

"The ocean," Ahli and Cyril said at the same time.

"Yes," Sadie said. "Now come on, we have to leave before they catch up to us."

Chapter 20

There was no dismay that compared to what Sadie felt when they finally got to the gate. They found out that the sensor to get in and out had been shot up and disabled. Even with both Cyril and Tyler, they were barely able to lift the heavy metal gate an inch. Olivette had set the perfect trap. There was nowhere for them to go but back.

Sadie didn't know what to do but blame herself. None of them would be in that situation had it not been for her money thirst. She clasped her hands together and put them on the back of her head while looking toward the sky.

"I know that look. Don't go blaming yourself," Tyler grabbed her hands from behind her head and held them in his. "We don't have time for that. We have to figure out a way to get out of here."

"But how?"

"We'll find a way. But for now, we need to get off the road. We're sitting ducks out here for those clucks to get us."

"Come on, let's go to the House of Greed," Rhonnie said, pointing at the second mansion a little ways away.

"We have to leave the truck," Cyril noted. "They'll know where to find us if we take it."

They started unloading the weapons, even Tyler, and Sadie made a face at him.

"Say, as much as I don't want to break the rules of this place, it feels like we have no choice," Tyler said.

"Yeah, boss. I don't think we have a choice," Rhonnie said, grabbing her own bag. "And if the Keepers or whoever were really here, wouldn't they have already punished Olivette? The bitch is on a rampage. What did we pack the guns for anyway?"

"In case we had to use them on the way here, not while we're here," Sadie said.

"Brayland said the only way he could put down the fiends on VEM was to shoot them in the head," Ahli told Sadie. "So unless you can come up with a better way, the next time one of those things comes at me, I'm putting two in their dome."

Sadie shook her head and grabbed her backpack before she walked away in a disappointed fashion. She refused to break the sacred rules of a place that had done nothing but feed her spirit. She had bonded with it. Nobody had broken the "neutral ground" law in decades, and she wouldn't be the one to taint the territory. To do so would be to break her own spirit.

When they got to the House of Greed, the smell hit them before they even saw the dead bodies strewn inside. The bellhop there had been murdered too, along with others. Sadie noticed how brutally they had been killed. Not with guns. Some looked as if they had been pummeled to death. Others had been stabbed with sharp objects. They found their way to the kitchen area, and they unloaded their weapons to count how much ammo they had.

"How many VEM heads did she have with her, Ahli?" Rhonnie asked.

"Maybe ten?"

"Ten superpowered druggies against five of us. One of whom is refusing to fight," Rhonnie said. "Great. This place is turning out to be my worst nightmare."

"You're not helping," Ahli told her and stood up. "I need to find some tape. I'm losing space on my belt for all my clips."

Sadie sat alone in the corner and watched her look around the kitchen for tape. Sadie was supposed to be their leader, but she was the only one sitting idle. She felt helpless. All she had wanted to do was come to Trap Street, destroy the formula, and then go home to administer the serum to whoever needed it.

"The serum," Sadie whispered to herself as if she had forgotten she even had it.

She put the backpack on her lap and unzipped it. Every syringe was still intact with the liquid inside of it. If there was a way that she could inject the serum into each of the soldiers Olivette brought with her, it would give them enough time to escape. But how? The gate was locked.

Her eyes fell on Rhonnie. Once, when Rhonnie had first come to stay with Sadie, she had tried to run off without telling anyone. She had overridden the security system and also the gate so that she could sneak out without being noticed. Sadie, of course, caught wind of it before she got too far. That was actually the reason Sadie started having her men physically man the gate.

Rhonnie looked up and saw that Sadie was eyeing her with a smile. "What did I do now?" Rhonnie asked guiltily.

"Do you remember when you overrode my security system at home?"

"Yeah. You almost killed me. I don't know what that has to do with this . . . wait." Rhonnie's eyes grew as she caught on to what Sadie was insinuating.

"If I asked you to override the sensor at the gate, do you think you could?"

"I . . . I don't know. The sensor at home was less advanced than the one here. Not only that, but I would need tools."

"These kinds of tools?" Ahli said from behind one of the counters in the kitchen. She had found a toolbox under one of the sinks and held it up.

"Yes, but—"

"Rhonnie, I need you," Sadie said seriously. "I think Olivette's plan to get out of here centered around the VEM heads she has with her. Tyler and Cyril might not have been able to lift the heavy gate, but ten of them could do it without breaking a sweat."

"Okay, but overriding that will take time. And I won't stand a chance out in the open with them out there."

"Yeah, and eventually they're gon' find us," Cyril said, clacking his gun. "But when they do, I'll be ready."

"With my plan, you won't even have to use guns," Sadie told them.

"How?"

"By sobering them up," she said, lifting up one of the syringes. "They can't hurt us if they're knocked out."

"But they have to get close enough for us to use those," Ahli pointed out.

"So we set a trap and lead them to us," Tyler said, standing up.

"And I have the perfect setup," Sadie said with a sly smile right before explaining to them what she needed them to do.

"Fuck!" Sadie exclaimed from the driver's seat of the Hummer.

She'd been in the process of moving the truck from the gate so Rhonnie could get to work on the sensor when it was time. When she was a few yards up the road from the House of Greed, she stopped to check her surroundings. It was so quiet that she could hear the sound of a twig breaking, except she didn't. She didn't notice the VEM heads approach the truck until it was too late. The driver's side window shattered, and she was dragged out of the vehicle by her hair.

"No! Let me go!" she shouted as she tried to fight their strong hands off.

She was no match for their strength, though. She was punched in the stomach so hard that it made her double over in agony. After that, she was lifted in the air and thrown violently to the ground. She put her hands up, preparing to block her face from their blows when a whistle sounded. Sadie lifted her head and saw Olivette walking toward them

"If you want any more of this, you'll back the fuck up," she sneered, shaking a large bag of VEM and aiming a gun their way.

They cowered like a group of animals so that Olivette could approach Sadie. She knelt beside her and snatched Sadie by her hair. The pain made Sadie wince, but she kept her eyes on Olivette's.

"Where are your friends?" Olivette asked.

"Hiding," Sadie answered.

"Why don't you tell them to come out if they want to save you?"

"They're not coming out until you leave," Sadie told her.

"I'm gonna find them and have them gutted alive," Olivette promised.

"Why would you do that if I'm giving you what you came all this way for?"

Olivette's eyes brightened slightly, but she didn't let go of Sadie's hair. She tightened her grip on it. Her look of happiness was quickly replaced with one of distrust.

"Why the switch-up?" she asked suspiciously.

"Because I'm going to strike a deal with you. You get the formula, and my friends walk out free."

"And why would I agree to such a thing?"

"Because I'm more than willing to die never telling you or anyone else where the formula is," Sadie said with her top lip curled.

She watched as Olivette weighed her choices before clenching her teeth together.

"Fine. As soon as you give me the formula, I'll leave."

"How do I know you'll make good on your word?"

"I'm a businesswoman at the end of the day," Olivette said with sincerity. "If you don't have trust among peers, where do you have it at all?"

Her expression was believable, so believable that Sadie reached for a piece of thick folded-up parchment that was tucked into the waist of her jeans. Olivette snatched it from her hand before it was even extended. She let Sadie's hair go and began to breathe wildly with excitement.

"Oh, my God. It's mine. It's finally mine!"

She stood up and kissed the paper. A hysterical laugh left her lips right before she pointed her gun at Sadie.

"I thought we had a deal," Sadie said in confusion.

"And you're a fucking idiot for believing me. If I broke the rules in a place this sacred, why do you think I would keep my word to you?"

Boom!

She fired the gun too quickly for Sadie to move out of the way. The bullet caught her in the shoulder, and blood splattered when it went through her back. The burning pain made Sadie's eyesight blurry, and she wanted to sprawl out on the ground. But she couldn't. She had to move, especially when she saw Olivette unfolding the paper. She was going to find out Sadie had given her a blank piece of parchment. Gripping her shoulder with her hand, Sadie stumbled to her feet.

"What is this? Where is the formula?"

Sadie was already running away from them. Although the VEM heads took off after her, she was thankful because they blocked Olivette's aim as she fired more shots. Sadie ran as fast as she could. She felt herself growing weak with each step she took, but she had to make it to the House of Greed. She was almost there . . . almost . . .

She fell through the front doors just when she thought she wasn't going to make it.

"Sadie!" she heard Ahli shout, but there was no time to help her.

Olivette's soldiers burst through the doors right after her, snarling, ready to rip her to shreds. Little did they know Tyler and Cyril were waiting for them. The first five came through the doors and didn't think to check their surroundings. They were only focused on where Sadie was scooting across the floor. Tyler and Cyril injected them with the serum, and like Ray had said, at first, they were disoriented, and then they passed out.

The next five weren't so easy, especially since Olivette entered the house, firing at will. Tyler and Cyril were too busy trying to inject the serum into the new soldiers while not getting killed in the process.

"I know the formula is here somewhere! And since you won't tell me, I'll kill all of you and look for it myself," Olivette shouted and pointed the gun at Sadie's head.

"Sike, bitch," Ahli said and swung a jab that caught Olivette hard on the side of her face.

The impact of the blow was enough to make Olivette drop the weapon, but not enough to take her off her feet. Sadie wanted to tell Ahli not to fight, but she barely had the energy to sit up. She watched helplessly as the two women fought in hand-to-hand combat. Ahli had power, but Olivette was small and had speed on her side. Ahli threw a punch and missed because Olivette ducked quickly out of the way. When she came back up, she delivered a vigorous uppercut to Ahli's chin, dazing her. Before Ahli could fall, Olivette grabbed her and placed her in a chokehold.

"Tell me where it is, or she dies," Olivette said breathlessly, facing Ahli toward Sadie.

"Don't," Ahli choked, gripping at Olivette's arm as it tightened.

"Tell me!" Olivette shouted in a fury. "I'm gonna kill her."

Sadie felt her heart breaking. She could literally see the strength leaving Ahli's body as her flailing legs slowed and her hands loosened their hold on Olivette's arm. When Sadie saw Ahli's eyes rolling, she'd had enough.

"Stop," she cried with tears falling from her eyes. "Let her go. I'll tell you where it is. Just don't kill her."

"Where is it?"

Sadie's eyes traveled across the room to where Tyler and Cyril were getting the serum. Sadie's bag was sitting on top of the front counter, and sticking out for everyone to see was a piece of parchment.

The second Olivette saw that, she couldn't care less about Ahli. She shoved her to the ground and ran toward it. When she had what she wanted, she exited the Greed House, leaving even her soldiers behind. Cyril had just stabbed Jaq, the last VEM head standing, in the neck with a syringe, making him drop like a fly.

Sadie used what little energy she had left to crawl toward Ahli and pull her head into her lap. She stroked her hair as Ahli coughed violently, and she let her tears fall freely. They had failed. Olivette had *Vita E Morte*.

"Sa . . . Sadie!" Ahli coughed violently as she gasped for air. "You should have let me die."

"I would never," Sadie said as her tears fell on Ahli's head. "You're my best friend . . . my sister."

In the distance, there was a woman's scream and a gunshot. Sadie's eyes went to the open door, and she abruptly remembered that only four of them were in the house.

"Oh, no. Rhonnie!"

Chapter 21

Twenty Minutes Earlier

"No matter what happens, I need you to get to that gate with those tools, do you understand me?" Sadie said from the front seat of the Hummer.

"Yeah, yeah, yeah," Rhonnie grumbled under her breath from the back-seat floor.

"I'm serious, Rhonnie."

"I know you are. I can't believe you're going to use yourself as bait. It's kind of gangster, but kind of stupid. You know? Maybe you should have made Tyler do it. I mean, he's bigger than you, and *kind* of disposable, you know? He did put a ring on another bitch's finger. If anybody deserves a VEM head beatdown, it's him."

Sadie glared back at Rhonnie in a way that made her throw her hands up in retreat. She knew she'd crossed the line with that one.

"I need you to shut up back there," Sadie said. "I don't need for Olivette to see me talking to you. You're not supposed to be in the car, remember? Fuck!"

"Shutting up now," Rhonnie said, again under her breath.

Rhonnie went back to lying as flat as she could in the back seat of the car. She also tried to breathe as quietly as possible, which was hard because the floor of the truck smelled like something had died back there. It felt like they had been waiting for ages, and she was about to pop back up and say something else when the glass of Sadie's window shattered. The defensive side in Rhonnie made her stick her head up, wanting to come to her aid, but Sadie saw her.

"No! Let me go!" Sadie shouted to her, and Rhonnie had no choice but to do as she said.

She let the VEM heads drag her through the window, and Rhonnie tried her best not to react when she heard the exchange between Sadie and Olivette. But the hardest thing to do was not hop out of the car when she heard the gunshot ring out, knowing it was Sadie who had gotten hit. Rhonnie prayed silently that she wasn't dead, and her prayers were answered.

"Get her! Don't let her get away!" Olivette shouted as she ran past the Hummer.

Rhonnie waited until she didn't hear any sounds outside, then lifted her head up. She watched as they all went inside the House of Greed, and when the coast was completely clear, she hopped in the driver's seat.

"It's gonna be just like hot-wiring a car," she told herself as she turned the Hummer around and drove for the gate.

As soon as she was there, she hopped out of the vehicle and got to work. The first thing she did was pop the top with a flat-head screwdriver that was in the toolbox. When the security cable and all the other wires were in her face, she closed her eyes and remembered everything her father had taught her about overriding security systems.

"Move quickly but delicately. Think of a security system as a bomb. The time is ticking, but if you fuck up, you're dead."

"'If you fuck up, you're dead,'" Rhonnie said, repeating her father's words aloud when she opened her eyes.

She grabbed a pair of pliers and disconnected one of the wires before replacing it with another one. She was so focused on what she was doing that she had beads of sweat dripping down her head. Her heart was trying to beat out of her chest as she connected the last two wires she needed together. To her delight, the gate started to rise instantly, and she let out a breath that she was holding in.

"Great, and here I was thinking that I was going to have to climb this gate," a voice said behind her, killing her happiness.

Rhonnie whipped around only to see Olivette standing there, pointing a gun at her and holding what looked like a bag of pills and a piece of paper.

"I got what I came for." Olivette glowered, waving the piece of paper. "*Vita E Morte* is mine!"

"No," Rhonnie shook her head in disbelief.

The only reason she could think of for Olivette to have the formula was if all of her friends were dead or badly hurt. She felt rage well up in her gut, and she made to charge at Olivette. But when the crazed woman cocked her gun, Rhonnie stopped after one step. All she had to defend herself were a couple of tools, and everybody knew you couldn't bring a screwdriver to a gunfight.

"I want to thank The Last Kings for their service," Olivette told her. "Soon, you will all answer to me!"

Rhonnie braced herself for the gunshot, but when it didn't come, she looked at Olivette, who seemed to be stuck in a trance. She was gawking in terror at something in the distance.

"You broke the rules," a voice that sounded like a loud whisper said behind Rhonnie.

Olivette's scream was high-pitched, and she averted the gun from Rhonnie and pointed it at whoever had spoken. She was able to fire once, but when the look of dread was still on her face, Rhonnie, who was frozen in fear, knew she had missed. As Olivette tried to shoot one more time, Rhonnie felt something smooth brush past her ear and saw it catch Olivette in the center of her forehead. It was a knife, and Olivette's eyes crossed as she tried to look at it, right before she fell dead to the ground.

Rhonnie's breathing was rigid. She was scared to see who was standing behind her. She could still feel their presence and didn't want to turn around to get a knife to the forehead too.

"W . . . who's there?" she found the courage to ask.

"A Keeper of this island," the whisper said, then grew silent.

Just like that, Rhonnie knew she was alone. She whisked around, and sure enough, there was nobody there. All she saw were trees blowing in the wind. She was still shaking by the time Ahli found her.

"Rhonnie!" Ahli screamed and threw her arms around her sister. "She got away before we could stop her. I . . . I thought you were dead."

"I thought y'all were dead." Rhonnie buried her head in her sister's neck and clung tightly to her.

When finally they let each other go, it was Cyril's turn to sweep her off her feet and into his arms. "I'm glad you're good, shorty. You had me worried for a second.

I see you worked your magic on the gate, too," he said, and then he noticed that she was shaking. He leaned back to study her. "You all right? That's not the first body you caught."

"You broke the rules," Sadie said, coming up to them. She was leaning on Tyler, who had tied his shirt tightly around her injured shoulder to stop the bleeding. "But you had to do what you had to do."

"But I . . . I didn't. I didn't kill her."

"What do you mean you didn't kill her, NaNa? She's dead," Ahli said, looking confused.

"I know, but I didn't do it," Rhonnie said, looking at all of them. "Sh . . . she was there pointing a gun at me one second, and the next, she had this look of fear in her eyes that I can't even explain to you. She tried to shoot something behind me, and whatever it was . . . it killed her."

While everyone else had confounded looks on their faces, Sadie took a good look at the knife in Olivette's head. Rhonnie followed her gaze to the handle of the knife, which was made out of what looked to be tree bark. Sadie gave an almost disbelieving chuckle.

"The Keepers of this island," she whispered. "They're real. I bet y'all are glad you listened to me."

"Hell yes!" Rhonnie exclaimed. "And now I want to leave and not come back for a long time."

"We have some unfinished business." Sadie winced as she took her backpack from Tyler and stepped away from him. She grabbed the bag of what was left of the VEM pills from beside Olivette's body as well as the formula to make them. "Can someone take me to the ocean, please?"

***

Rhonnie sat cross-legged on the beach next to Cyril as the sun started to set on the water, and it was so mesmerizing, even more so since they'd all almost lost their lives. They watched Sadie and Ahli tie a heavy rock to the piece of parchment that had caused them all so much trouble and throw it into the ocean. They contemplated throwing the pills in the ocean too, but they didn't want the fish to swallow them. So instead, they started a bonfire and burned them all. They figured it wasn't breaking the rules since the pills were never stored on Trap Street.

Tyler stood at the end of the dock and waved at a boat that was speeding their way, and Rhonnie was relieved that it was over.

"A stack for your thoughts?" Cyril asked, nudging her with his shoulder. "You've been real quiet this whole time."

"If I tell you, you really better give me a stack when we get back to the States."

"I got you."

"I'm just thinking about how relieved I am that this is over," Rhonnie told him. "And I'm wondering who's going to clean up the mess we left."

"The Keepers of the island," Cyril said, making his voice go sarcastically deeper.

"You get on my nerves," Rhonnie said with a laugh. "But for real, that bitch Olivette was nuts. I'm glad we made it out of there in one piece."

"Hell yeah, me too. If I had known all this was gon' happen when you called me into your city—"

"You wouldn't have come?" she interrupted him.

"Man, I don't know," Cyril answered honestly. "But that's just the way the universe works. Sometimes we aren't supposed to have a choice."

"That's just part of the design," she said, and he smiled down at her.

"Now you're getting it."

"What are you going to do when you get back to L.A.?" she asked, resting her head on his shoulder.

"Send for you." He grabbed her hand in his. "I think it's only fair I show you how we get down after you took me on this exciting adventure. Come on, the boat is almost here."

He helped her to her feet, but he didn't let go of her hand until they reached where Ahli and Sadie were. They were holding hands as well, and when they saw Rhonnie approaching, Ahli reached out her other hand.

"I'm sorry, partna, but I need my sister," she said to Cyril.

"I don't want no smoke," he said, giving Rhonnie a wink.

He started to join Tyler on the dock, but Sadie stopped him. The two exchanged a knowing look, which left Rhonnie confused.

"I put it back," Cyril told her.

"Good. What was it?"

"A pendant. It was something he never took off when we were kids. When I saw it in the room, I just couldn't help myself. It brought back so many good memories. Shit, I thought I forgot," Cyril answered, and Rhonnie suddenly understood. He wasn't allowed to take anything from the island. "How did you know I took something?"

"Because if I were in your position, I would have been tempted to as well," Sadie stated. "Cane left his things here for a reason, though, and no matter how hard it is to, you have to respect it."

"And I always know where to find them," he said. "But I'll let y'all have your *Waiting to Exhale* moment," he joked. "I'm about to go chop it up with Tyler about how he owes me a hundred K when we get back. I got six of them niggas back there, and he only got four. Ay, Tyler! Run me my money!"

They laughed as he walked off, and when he was gone, they went back to staring at the water. Despite the utter chaos that had just transpired, Rhonnie had never felt such tranquility. She didn't know if it was the sound of the waves or if it was because she was standing there with her sisters.

"I love the two of you like my own flesh and blood," Sadie said, breaking the silence in a shaky voice. "I met you by chance, but you have become my sisters by choice. Today, I thought I lost both of you, and it felt like I was suffocating. It would have been my fault, and I wouldn't be able to carry that with me. Because of that, I'm releasing you from being my personal security."

"What, bitch?" The words just slipped out of Rhonnie's mouth, and she cleared her throat to correct herself. "What I mean is, you can't *release* us from doing something we choose to do. Shit, just give a bitch a few more days off and we can call it even."

"Yeah, plus you pay too good, and we're technically dead, remember? They don't even hire corpses at McDonald's," Ahli said, giving her a look like she had just said the most preposterous thing. "And if you hire someone else full-time, I would be too worried about you. So that's sweet of you to say, but nope. Plus, we *didn't* die *because* we have each other. We're a team."

"Forever," Rhonnie said.

"Okay." Sadie blinked her eyes feverishly as she stared at the two of them lovingly.

The tears sliding down her face caused the ones in Rhonnie's eyes, and before they knew it, they were huddled together crying. On the dock, Tyler and Cyril were staring at them, shaking their heads.

"Okay, come on," Ahli said, waving her hands down her face. "Nathaniel is back with the boat. We have to get back to Antigua so Sadie can get some medical attention."

"I'll be fine to fly back home," Sadie tried to convince her and motioned to the backpack on her back. "I need to get this serum to Nebraska."

"We can mail it! But you're going to the hospital, and that's that on that."

The two of them went back and forth all the way up until they got on the boat. Cyril and Tyler were already on board, and Rhonnie let them go before her. The first thing Ahli did was put on a life jacket, which Rhonnie found funny. She was still terrified of the ocean after the horrors they had just faced.

When Nathaniel held out a hand to help Rhonnie, the wind blew on her neck and made her look back past the ocean shore and into the trees. Her eyes might have been playing tricks on her, but she could have sworn she saw an island woman looking directly at her, wearing leaves as a dress. But when Rhonnie blinked, she was gone.

"Miss?"

Rhonnie turned her attention back to Nathaniel and his awaiting hand. She grabbed it and climbed on board the chartered boat. Before he sailed away from the dock, he looked at them and seemed to take notice of the blood and bruises they all had.

"An exciting time on Hustle Island?" he asked with a raised eyebrow.

The five of them looked at each other as if debating whether to tell him what had transpired.

"No," Sadie answered for all of them. "Let's just say it was more like a nightmare on Trap Street."

The End